POWDER MONKEY

Powder Monkey

Adam Hardy

NEW ENGLISH LIBRARY
TIMES MIRROR

To Victor Briggs, a fellow-writer

An NEL Original
© Adam Hardy 1973

*

FIRST NEL PAPERBACK EDITION NOVEMBER 1973

*

NEL Books are published by
New English Library Limited from Barnard Inn, Holborn, London, E.C.1,
Made and printed in Great Britain by Hunt Barnard Printing Ltd., Aylesbury, Bucks.

45001621 8

Chapter One

George Abercrombie Fox attended Tyburn for his uncle's execution warmly snugged in his mother's womb.

Mary knew she was near her time.

The boisterousness of the crowds, the constant activity, the calls of the vendors touting their wares and crying up oranges and apples and sweetmeats, the screams of lost children, the barking of dogs half-crazy in the prevailing excitement, the tramp and shuffle of hundreds of pairs of feet, the hot yet sultry and miasmic atmosphere, all combined to dizzy her. But nothing in the busy scene so daunted her as the gaunt mute arms of the scaffold.

Six years ago the old permanent gallows had been removed and the new movable scaffold had been pressed into service.

Today there was little of the pomp of a great execution, nothing like the rituals surrounding the hanging, five years ago, of Earl Ferrers, for Abercrombie Fox although condemned as a highwayman, was merely a mean dockyard labourer.

Rather, as Mary knew with a fierce resentful bitterness, he had been a dock labourer, like his brother John, Mary's husband.

The ever-present stinks of life were familiar to Mary Fox and her nose seemed able of its own accord to adjust to foetid pollution; but the pressing unwashed bodies all about clammied her in a vapour of vomit. She began to feel faintness.

Only a petty misdemeanour it had been, a trifling lapse of duty in which he had been found out, that had brought to Abercrombie Fox instant dismissal. All his attempts to regain honest employment had been fruitless. As John Fox's older brother he had refused all offers of help – for, truth to tell, the Foxes could barely scrape a subsistence for themselves – and so abject starvation and misery had inevitably followed.

But the Foxes were of a breed of people who would not bow the knee to fate. They would never succumb without a struggle; they would continue right to their last breath.

Abercrombie Fox had turned highwayman out of desperation and fear and need.

'Careful of my wife, cully!' roared John Fox, pushing savagely at a stumbling, bottle-waving oaf who almost toppled Mary over.

'Make him dance!' the drunk was bawling, hiccoughing. 'Let's see him dangle!'

Mary clasped her first-born, John, to her breast. He rested there, comfortably ensconced over the proud swell of her stomach. She almost fell, stumbling, then she felt the strong grip of her husband about her, supporting her.

The drunk staggered on. The baying noise of the waiting crowd, waiting for Death, beat in insufferably upon Mary.

'I shouldn't have come, John – '

'Aye, Mary, my love. I think perhaps you had better not. But we're here now, and poor Abe will dangle soon.'

'Poor Abe!'

'You are – all right, Mary?' John Fox looked at his wife with a sudden startlement. Truth to tell, having a brother hanged was as wonderfully concentrating to the mind as being a father for the second time. Mary looked white, peaky.

'I don't know, John – '

Mary had insisted on going to the execution. She and John taking turns to carry little John had tramped with friends and dockyard mateys all the way up from the eastern end of London Town. She went out seldom enough from their row-hovel and had resented in a wild fruitless way that her brother-in-law should thus furnish the excuse for an expedition. But with a fierceness that met and matched that of her husband with a darker pride that flowed more sullenly beneath his high temper, she had made up her mind to go. Once Mary Fox made up her mind it remained made up. Married at seventeen, a mother at eighteen, and now expecting her second child at nineteen, she was unlikely to be put off by mere physical discomfort.

The September day lowered about her. The smells and the sweating stinks, the noise, the incessant movement, all dinned it seemed straight into her brain. The crowds grew more restless. Fights broke out and were settled with a man on the ground

6

clasping his guts and another roaring his laughter, and strutting, and drinking again.

From all the houses and stands around, along the crossroads, where seats cost what a working man earned in a year, the Fashion watched, pomanders to noses, waiting for the delectable spectacle of a fellow human being dancing on air with his neck caught in the nine-knotted loop.

Mary knew nothing of them. Again she stared with a sick and frightened loathing, a fascinated revulsion, on the old dark beams of the scaffold. On the platform men in sombre black stood, waiting. There was a bible, a prayer-book, up there, held daintily between soft white hands. The scarlet of soldiers ranked solidly in precise lines and everyone present knew with an empty darkness of the soul that these soldiers would fire their muskets and use their bayonets should their officers in the brave gold-laced coats and cocked hats so order.

Still holding Mary, John Fox saw Perkin Adams push through the outskirts of the crowd, glance about, and then run across.

'You'd best stay here, John, with Mary –'

'No, Perkin –' John Fox said, at once, and then pressed and looked at his wife. He had planned to take his place in the forefront, right up against the scaffold, to pay a proper last respect to his elder brother. But Mary worried him. She smiled and squeezed his arm.

'Yes, John, dearest. Do you go on. I will be all right.'

Perkin Adams, one of the dockyard workers who had tramped up here with the Foxes, a squat square man with labourer's shoulders, dressed like them all in rough clothes that were, in God's truth, his best, pursed his lips and shook his head.

John and Abercrombie were brothers – more, they were friends.

'I had best stay with you, Mary.'

'No, John! If Abercrombie looks down from the – ' She hesitated, and then jerked her round chin up. 'If Abercrombie looks down from the scaffold and does not see you, dearest, he will believe we have deserted him.'

'We'll be there, Mary,' said Perkin Adams, a trifle uncomfortably. He let his eyes swivel to take a sidelong glance at Mary's swollen stomach. 'We'll give him a proper send off.'

'John . . .'

John Fox returned the pressure of his wife's hand. Then he

took a decision typical of the Foxes, pragmatical, hard, common-sense. He spoke firmly, so as to show he meant what he said and would stand no nonsense.

'Abe will know we will never forget him. He has been a good brother. But you are alive and he will soon be dead. My duty is to you, now, Mary – you and the child. We must look forward – '

Underlining the practicality of his words a fluttering racing mob of half-drunken men and women crashed past, seeking a better vantage point, hallooing, waving bottles. John Fox pulled his pregnant wife out of their way. One of the roisterers, whose flushed face and swollen nose spoke eloquently of deep indulgence in spirits of all kinds, running and staggering along in the wake of his friends, collided with Perkin Adams, bounced, tripped, sprawled forward. He lost his bottle and grabbed for support.

John Fox saw that the nearest support would be the long dress Mary wore. Without hesitation John moved forward, brought his knee up, smashed that hard and boney object into the drunk's face. The man squealed and collapsed sideways.

Blood spurted from his mangled nose.

Perkin Adams laughed.

'You've tapped his claret, John! Drunken whoreson.'

'I can't leave Mary now, Perkin. If you can – shout up to Abercrombie. Tell him – tell him –' John Fox's hard and care-lined face could not soften, even at this moment; instead he became harder still, tough and revengeful. 'Tell him we will remember him always.'

'Aye, John. I'll do that.'

And Perkin Adams pushed back into the crowd, to bludgeon his way to the front, shouting a clear way to the dockyard mateys clustered in the front of the mob.

Mary clung to her husband and felt – and felt the shooting and yet expanding pain cleave her.

'Oh – John!'

'Mary?'

'It's – gone now. Look, dearest, what is that man in black doing now?'

The answer came in a sudden stillness. The crowd fell silent. A sharp screech, then a click, and then a thudding crash. The crowd huzzaed their approval.

'The executioner is testing the drop, dear.'

'Yes – '

Earl Ferrers, it had been, who was first hanged by the use of the drop, five years ago in 1760, and the novelty of the device had still not worn off. Felons could now be gibbetted by statute law, or dissected by the surgeons, and whatever happened to Abercrombie Fox was out of the hands of unimportant people like dockyard labourers, relatives or no. Abercrombie would have rough hemp around his neck to take his life. Earl Ferrers, so the broadsheets said, had been favoured with a silken rope.

The crash of testing the drop with that ominous double clatter, drove a spike of fresh agony into Mary. She gasped. At once John took little John from her, concerned, looking about for help. Young himself, barely twenty two, he had already gone through the miserable process of becoming a father, and could recognise the signs. The old crone back home by the Thames-side marshes had warned them that the second baby would come quicker than the first.

'I think, John, dearest – it is coming – I did not – '

'Hush, hush.'

The crowds had resumed their raucous yelling and singing, their drinking and quarrelling, and there would be no help there.

Now Mary was clutching herself. She knew, with a sudden and desperate fear, that she had miscalculated. More probably, the excitement, the fear, the constriction of the surroundings, were bringing her contractions on early. She knew.

'I must lie down.'

John with little John on his left arm guided his wife away from the crowd. A house ahead with a door open might offer shelter, surely, no one would refuse them?

But –

'Away, away! Clear off! This is a respectable house!'

The man, fat in long blue coat and fawn breeches, his face bulbous with apoplectic anger, shook a stick at them. The knob of the stick gleamed dully gold.

'But – my wife! I need help!'

'Then seek it elsewhere, you scum of the gutter!'

Two houses John Fox tried after that, and at each door he was turned away. No one wanted anything to do with gutter

9

scum dragged from their hovels by a hanging.

'You should not have brought your wife! Disgusting! No better than animals!' The reactions of these people brought near despair to John Fox. But he would not tamely submit.

'My child is not to be born in a gutter, no matter he may live there all his life!' he shrieked, and tried to force his way into the doorway where brawny arms and well-fed bodies ejected him with a casual brutal force.

Had he been wearing a good broadcloth coat, with silver buttons, and a fancy waistcoat, glitteringly white shirt and lace, boots polished to a gleaming blackness, then they would have welcomed him in, and the women of the household would have run to help and cooed over Mary, instead of glaring with greedy eyes from the upper windows upon the gaunt black arms of the gallows tree.

Although – they might not. They would have ordered their servants to care for Mary until the execution was over. For babies were born every day, it was mere routine; a hanging was after all something of a speciality among treats.

A choked scream broke from Mary.

'John!'

He tried to support her but her legs gave way. She collapsed. Wildly he glared about. Blood drummed in his head. He could hear over the crowd noises a great whooshing as though the Angel of Death beat his wings triumphantly above.

'You are taking one life this day!' he screamed. 'You shall not have two more.'

The walk up to Tyburn early had masked the first stage of labour. Now the second was upon Mary and, with a swiftness frightening and yet reassuring, the second was upon her.

Reassuring – for she was very young, and healthy and in full strength and used to hard work, so that the baby should come swiftly and cleanly without complications.

But, for all that, as John Fox fought wildly for help, Mary lay in the gutter and felt the pincer-pangs cleaving her and shuddered to each successive shock of contraction, swifter and swifter, fiercer and fiercer, agony piled upon agony.

John Fox could waste time no longer upon these scions of the upper classes, gawping at a hanging, callously uncaring of the plight of his wife. He ran towards the crowd, and when he saw whom he sought he plunged in, thrusting bodies aside mercilessly – uncaring in his turn.

He grasped the arm of the plump goodwife and swung her about.

'Please! You must help me! My wife – '

The beldame stared at him as though he was drunk, like so many gathered here. Her fat cheeks quivered. Her eyes, so like the currants in buns the Foxes saw seldom, sized up this husky young man in his shabby best. She saw the distraught terror upon his face, the beseeching glaze in his eyes.

'Come quickly, please, I beg of you – '

'Whisht awhile, young man.' She spoke quickly in the ear of the stout man, shabbily although cleanly turned out, at her side. He looked grave; but nodded his assent. Urgently, then, John Fox led the woman to where Mary lay, breathing in great gasping heaves, and quivering, and trembling, her knees bent, her black skirts dragged up. The woman let out a cry of horror. She darted forward.

'May the Good Lord ha' mercy on the poor child! The bairn's nigh here!'

A tremendous shout went up from the crowd.

Instinctively, John swung about, knowing what that great cry meant; but from here he could not see his brother being led out for his last walk.

The sonorous gong note of a church bell broke over the bedlam and was met by the instant changing of the roaring into a demoniac cheer.

'A quarter of an hour to go, lads!'

The woman was bending over Mary. Mary's skirts were pushed right back. One or two onlookers looked back, over their shoulders; and then faced front again. Babies – what were babies beside a hanging?

'Don't stand there like a loon, laddie! Run and fetch hot water to wash the bairn! The varmint's almost here – '

John Fox ran.

The inn, where the landlord had contemptuously thrust him back, would not refuse to sell him hot water. If the fat slug did, then John vowed to thrust his knuckles down the man's throat.

In the front ranks of the crowd a knot of men clad in the shabby and rough although clean clothes of their best surged forward. Their faces were congested with the frustrated anger

11

that availed nothing against musket and bayonet. They were the dockyard mateys, up to see a comrade hanged. They shouted and shook their fists as Abercrombie was led up on to the scaffold.

A gold-laced officer snapped a command and the soldiers stiffened.

The moment, trembling with ugly tensions, might have snapped into violent action; but Ambercrombie Fox drew himself up and shouted down.

'Avast there, mateys! I wouldn't have another man's wife widdered on account o' me! I thank you for being here – John?'

He looked down, did Abercrombie, searching among that excited mass of faces for the familiar features of his younger brother. A fine tall man, Abercrombie; broad of shoulder and with the beaked and arrogant nose of the Foxes. He looked –

'Mary's near her time, Abercrombie!' roared up Perkin Adams. 'They're here, both on 'em! Mary dropping just about now, I reckon.'

The shouts and catcalls now drowned out any rational conversation. The officials prepared to go about their work.

And over all the great bell gonged towards the moment of execution.

Considerable feeling had been aroused over the fate of Abercrombie Fox. Destitute but proud, he had refused offers of assistance and taken himself to the trade of a gentleman of the road. But, his first, out west of Hammersmith, had resulted in abject failure and ignominious arrest. He had never been a true highwayman, his heart had not been in the transaction, and he had offered no resistance.

But, even then, his sentence had not been commuted to transportation, as it might well have been, and he was condemned to be hanged.

The bell crashed out relentlessly.

For fifteen minutes before the execution to fifteen minutes afterwards that brazen tongue would declare to the listening world what was going forward, here at Tyburn Tree.

Clutching an immense and steaming copper pan John Fox hurried back to Mary.

He had been faced with a choice few men are called upon to make.

He could have gone to see his brother hanged and left his

12

wife to labour in childbirth alone; or he could have stayed by her and let his brother dangle on air alone.

What alternatives!

But he had taken the course he believed to be the right one, and now there was no drawing back.

Being the man he was, of stock noted for the stubborn obduracy, the sheer bull-dog tenacity, of the blood-line, he thrust away all thoughts about what might have been. Now only Mary mattered, she and the baby so soon to be born into this cruel and turbulent world.

Mary, awash on a sea of pain, and yet scarcely comprehending that the sea both bore her up and surged over her, lost and seized in the culminating moments of bringing forth a new life, screamed and bit down on the lump of rag clamped between her teeth. The crowd roar, bestial in its growling undertones, swamped everything – and then, as though chopped on a butcher's block, ceased.

Absolute silence engulfed Tyburn.

The great bell tolled.

The hateful screeching slide of levers, the double clack-clack of the trap, the drop opening – and –

The mass roar broke out into a bedlam eruption of noise.

'He's gone!'

And, from the woman bending over Mary:

'He's arrived.'

Together, then, like ships passing on reciprocal bearings, Abercrombie Fox passed out of this life and his nephew entered it, squalling.

The woman was doing quick and competent things with the hot water, and rags torn from Mary's petticoats, there was the flash of a pair of pocket-scissors, there was blood staining the cobbles of the gutter. Mary lay limply. The woman straightened up and her face, flushed and with strands of hair draggling across her forehead, showed clearly the light of pride in accomplishment.

'I'll stay by her, young man, see the afterbirth comes away clean. Take your son – '

Dumbly, John Fox took the yelling scrap of pink humanity in his arms. He looked down at his eldest son, John, and then back again to little John's brother. 'George,' he said. 'We agreed to call him after Mary's father, if he was a boy.'

13

Looking up at her husband, Mary found a small smile. She felt the emptiness after the pain. 'George,' she said. 'But, dear heart – think – when he was born – poor Abe – '

John nodded.

'Yes, Mary. It would be fitting. Our son shall be called George Abercrombie Fox.'

So it was that Fox went to Tyburn Tree warmly snugged in the womb of his mother, and was there pitched into this vale of tears, brought forth by a hanging, and born in the gutter.

Chapter Two

Following the dramatic entrance of George Abercrombie Fox into life a number of years passed before Mary had Susan, her eldest daughter, and after her birth there followed year by year, a regular appearance of children, so that in all thirteen were born to John and Mary Fox. Of these only three died in infancy, a testament in an age of terrifying infant mortality at once to the care and love lavished upon them by their parents as much as to their natural health and resilience.

Fox grew up sturdy, loving an open-air life, independent to the point of being, in the words of those who crossed his path, bloody-minded. Carefree with the few precious years of early childhood he quickly came to understand the problems confronting the Fox family, the grinding poverty, the never-ending effort to scrape a crust, the daily fears for the father's health and the father's chances of work. With his brother John he would fight and quarrel, would go for long walks, would talk with the terse loquacity of siblings close together in feeling of their plans and dreams. By the time he was four he had seen three killings, although not fully understanding why one of the men fighting had fallen down, spilling blood, and wouldn't get up again. The fourth time – a drunken brawl in which a jaggedly broken gin bottle carved a seaman's face into red gristle – he understood. And the next fight in which he and John were involved with the Hogan brothers from the next street witnessed young Fox taking a broken bottle to them. They fled.

Fox learned quickly.

Brother John was never as robust or as animal-like in his health and spirits as George Abercrombie. Always a pallor clung about his face, lending a nimbus-effect to his skin. His eyes, though, were very beautiful.

During this piping time of peace the Royal Navy was, as usual, allowed to decay. Work in the dockyards was hard to come by. Mary, with a tightening of her lips, planned how best to cope with the weekly disasters and crises, and if she regretted that she had married a man without a trade in his hands, she never showed it. That it rankled was perfectly clear in the way in which she had early determined that her son should learn a trade, have the possibility of life in his own hands. John should be a carpenter in the yards. Even now, during this time of peace when the King did not need his ships, carpenters were still working where mere labourers might beg a crust. If they tried to steal a crust – well, Uncle Abercrombie pointed the end of that.

'My mother told me what happened to Grandfather Blake after he had learned his trade,' she said to her husband. 'But they will always want carpenters.'

Blake had been her mother's name, she was a Lovett. John Fox had heard the story, of how old Blake, as a young man, had apprenticed to the wood-carvers, had learned how to carve so beautifully that one could swear a cherub or a mermaid, a horse or a dolphin, was truly alive, springing flesh and blood from the stern-galleries of a first-rate. Then, after the scandal of the costs of decorations to *Royal Sovereign* in 1701, which included a fanciful allegorical concotion, the Lords of the Admiralty, frightened, ordered that in future all decorations of carving must be restricted to the beakhead and stern galleries. Old Blake had been summarily pitchforked out of work. He had scraped a living carving for churches and had survived; but his daughter had drummed into her daughter that if a man chose a trade – as any sensible man must – let him choose one that would not melt beneath his feet like the polar icebergs.

Her mother had married her cousin – hence the same name – and this ancestry, to which young Fox listened avidly, was reasonably clear; but the rest of the blood lines that had culminated in him were far less clear. From the earliest age he felt, somehow, that he was destined to do something special in this life, some vast and obscure undertaking that he could never specify much less comprehend; and if he did not spend over-long in day-dreaming this was simply because he was not afforded the time or opportunity.

16

So brother John was to apprentice as a carpenter, the money would be found, Mary his mother would see to that, and brother George, because he loved his brother despite their wrangling and their fighting, wanted desperately to help in whatever way he could. For brother John would bring back good fortune to the Foxes, give them the security a labouring job could never bring.

Even though Fox could always, when they were grown to a size, best him, John was still sturdy enough among the children swarming barefoot and in rags along the waterfront, skylarking on the mudflats, sailing in crazy old patched-up tubs that were barely seaworthy. They formed a duo, did John and George Fox. The Hogan brothers from the next street trod warily when the Foxes were abroad, and the children's gangs engaged with blood-curdling cries between the wooden houses, leaning lopsided against their ship-timbers supports, creaking in the wind.

During this time Fox went through a strange experience with old Makepeace, the sexton, that he did not understand at all. He kicked Makepeace where experience had told him a man would be hurt, and ran off. Only in afteryears was the inner truth of that episode vouchsafed Fox.

In after years he was able to look back with eyes that grim experience had opened and see, with a fresh and horrified comprehension, what his life as a marshboy along the Thames had truly been like.

At the time he snapped up all that life offered him as one of the mangy cur-dogs would snap up one of the myriads of sleek fat rats that infested the houses and yards.

Over everything hung the tang of water and mud, of tar and sulphur, of the reek of huddled humanity.

Very early Fox came to disregard what the weather might do to him. He went everywhere barefoot – shoes were items of apparel strange and remote – dressed in a tattered red shirt and a pair of breeks cut down from a corpse washed up on the mud, breeks that Mary had bargained passionately for and gained with the addition of her sweet smile to the pennies so carefully counted out. She had won the corpse's breeks over the opposition of Mrs Hogan, a harridan with stringy black hair and a tongue like a viper, who coveted them for her Patrick. How Fox crowed when he pulled them on, after Mary had cut and sewn them, gleeing over this further discomfiture of the hated Hogans!

Rain, snow, hail, sleet, none made him overtly discomfited, although his feet, tough and calloused though they were, might turn blue. Somehow into his breeding had gone the strength necessary, and early understanding that this was his life had toughened him against giving way to feelings of cold and pain. When his father leathered him, as he did from time to time when Fox had performed something so outrageous that punishment fitting must be administered, he could withstand the blows with a resigned fatalism that powerfully affected his father. John Fox loved his family, and his chastisements, though just, were invariably meted out in accordance with a scale that gave favour to those whose sins were least.

The sight of ships' masts greeted him from the moment he stepped out of the door, and always, the talk was of ships and of cables, timber and trenails, Stockholm tar and painting and paying. The Thames-side docks dominated and controlled and consumed the lives of the men and women in their huddled houses, and of their children also.

The first time Fox fell in he moved his arms and legs in automatic reflex and found he could keep his head above the murky water. He could never remember a time when he had not been able to swim. Stark naked he and the others of the gang would dive and disport themselves, until chased off by some stick-waving red-faced adult, for whom they entertained the liveliest antipathy and who they insulted with all the invective of their seniors.

Along in the Rotherhithe yards they were building ship-rigged sloops, vessels pierced with ten gun ports a side, to be classed as sixth-rates. Everybody got blind drunk at each launching. Crime appealed to Fox only if it could serve some useful end. He had seen the dreadful effects on those who had been caught, and he had early vowed never to share their fate. So it was that he was more circumspect and more astute than others at removing the drunks' silk kerchiefs, a watch if he was lucky, any property that was not chained to the drunk's body.

An epic contest ensued one launching when the Foxes and the Hogans clashed over a Navy Surveyor who fell down dead drunk outside the *Crown*. Silk kerchief ripped into two, a gilt-buckled shoe to the Hogans and the other to the Foxes, half a hat to each family, an embroidered coat ripped up and a linen shirt ripped into shreds – by the time they were through little was gained and much gore was spilt; but for George and John Fox the game had been worth it, for the Hogans, Patrick – he who had been breekless for a fortnight – Shaun and Mick had been seen off in a fashion at once grand and satisfying.

Strangely enough it was Katie Hogan, the sister of the deadly enemy, who first felt Fox's fingers upon her, and lifted her ripe lips for a kiss. Fox experienced the most intense astonishment at this; but was nothing loth, Hogan or not. He had early found that to refuse an opportunity in this life meant almost certainly that the opportunity would never offer again.

By this time the little wooden row house with its warm and comforting smells of cooking and friendly humanity was filling up with the Fox children. Regular employment for a remarkably long spell had given John Fox the opportunity to rent another room in the house; but still they slept crammed into two rooms, with the kitchen as a bedlam of confusion and strife, of laughter and of tears.

One day Fox spied his father in close converse with the Hogan father, a dreaded Ogre who would lash out at a Fox child as soon as spit, and marvelled. The upshot of that conversation did not occur to him for many years.

His mother's sister, Elizabeth Lovett, came to stay with the Foxes. Unmarried, anxious about life, Elizabeth was to help in the house. The help was welcome; but the overcrowding was thereby the worse.

When Fox was told by his parents what plans they had laid for him he was incredulous, mutinous, near to tears – for he never cried, considering that to be girls' work – and thoroughly upset.

'But, George, dear – it will be a lovely change.'

'I don't wanna leave you – '

'Now, George!' said his father.

Fox knew that tone of voice. It rumbled low, softly and yet firmly final. It meant: 'You may be a young rip but I'm your father and I know what's best for you. You will!'

'But Uncle Ebeneezer!'

Fox had heard of Uncle Ebeneezer. He lived right out on the marshes, a widower with a son and daugher, reputed to be a man taciturn and isolated, a man whose life revolved around his punt, his punt-gun and the seabirds who filled his days with clamour and movement and profit.

'He's your great uncle and he's a man to be reckoned with, George.' His father put a hand on Fox's head as he spoke and ruffled the thick brown hair. 'You behave yourself, mind. No skylarking where it'll harm him – and if you touch his punt-gun I'll personally stripe you so – '

'All right, John, dear, all right!' Mary cast a look at her husband and then smiled at her son. 'I know George won't disgrace us.'

This injunction put Fox into an unenviable position; for he had immediately promised himself a thorough investigation of this awe-inspiring punt-gun of Uncle Ebeneezer's. As it was, it had been forbidden him, and young rascal though he was, a very rogue of rogues, he would obey the injunctions of his parents. Experience had taught him that they knew what they were talking about. But, still and all – if he could just fire it off once! It would make the most glorious bang. That he knew with a conviction that began at his scalp and tingled out through his toenails.

By the prodigious achievements of mothers that make of them miracle-workers, Mary carefully gathered together a spare shirt – a blue one, with a bright check patch over the heart without enquiring too closely how the hole had come just so ominously there – and an old wrap-rascal coat of frieze that was more darns and patches than coat. His father gave him a belt with a buckle that Fox promised would shine like gold after he had finished with it. And then, moment supreme! his father solemnly produced a leather sheath, and in the sheath, a knife – a real steel knife, a real knife, a sailor's knife, a true sailor's steel knife with a wooden and leather handle, a knife, a real knife – *his* knife!

Slowly, holding his breath, Fox drew the blade from the sheath.

He looked at it.

Mary looked at her son's face, and she lifted the corner of her apron, and then started in scolding Fox, for the Foxes were a people whose feelings ran deep.

But – a knife!

'Wear it just to the right of your backbone, over the hip,

George. Any man must have a knife. 'Tis a law of nature.'

None of the Foxes was literate, of course; but John had taken Mary about, when they'd been courting, and they both loved the roll of a fine phrase. If they had ever had the chance to read, they both knew in some subconscious and resigned way, they would have found a wider, more brightly-coloured, view on life. As it was, a knife was the finest thing a young man could have.

'Jest remember, George, if you have to stick a man.' His father looked down very gravely upon him now. 'Make sure it is all you can do, that there's nothin' else, nary other a way out. Killin' is something you don't want to do unless you mean it. And if you do mean it, then have a damn good reason for it – '

'John!' said Mary. But she did not pursue her comment, either on the sentiment or the language. She understood this was a matter between father and son.

'And if you do mean it, and have a good reason to do it, then, my lad, *do* it! Don't shilly-shally – if'n you do, you'll be the one kilt! Got it, lad?'

'Aye, father,' said young Fox.

Saying goodbye to the children was hard enough, saying goodbye to his father and mother was a torture, and saying goodbye to brother John made him feel a traitor.

'Them Hogans, Johnny – '

'I'll burn and sink 'em, Abe! There's Peter and Charlie and the two Gibson kids – we're all gonna stick together more'n ever now – ' The whole gang knew who was the fiercest fighter, the toughest opponent, the one no Hogan alone, or in pairs or, even, in triples, would willingly face. George Abercrombie's fists and calloused feet and broken bottle were going to be missed.

He wrapped his worldly possessions in a red and white checked kerchief and John found a stick to thrust through the knot. He cocked it over his shoulder and the bundle slanted up impudently. He looked up at his father. It was spring time, and the buds were bursting and the last frost was gone, and the air breathed sweet and bracing, odoriferous with the everlasting tang of mud and water.

'I'll be back day after next, Mary,' said her husband as she clasped her son in her arms. She was pregnant, of course. This was a normal and natural state of affairs, this sending of a child

21

to live with relatives, a custom common to the period; but she was all one ache and longing for her George Abercrombie, her son born in the gutter at an execution.

They set out walking, for they could not afford the carrier, swinging along, father and son, into the early spring weather. Fox kept touching the knife at his hip. Now he had started, he was avaricious for the adventures to come.

He was just eight years old.

He felt like King George himself.

Chapter Three

Fox grew to know and love the sea birds of the marshes and river.

And yet –

'Grab him, Abe, afore he gits away!'

Jake Fox, his rough red face excited, his eyes alive with the chase, roaring him on, and Fox flinging himself forward to slide squishing through the mud, bending the reed stems, and so grip his fingers around the bird's legs with the desperate clutch of the drowning man.

The bird threshed his wings, squawking, his orange beak opening wickedly. Fox held on, and scrabbled up, and dragged the bird down and so broke its neck. He looked back at Jake. Jake shouted and waved his black kerchief.

'Well done, young 'un!'

They both slithered and slipped back from the water-gleaming mud on to firmer land. Jake felt the bird, running his broad brown hands with their black and broken finger-nails over the white feathers of the breast. He chuckled.

'She's a fine fat 'un, Abe. Dad might knock 'em outta the sky by the score with his gun – but we can choose the best, eh, lad?'

They began to walk back, alertly on the lookout. Around them the marshes stretched, flat and level and shining with the colours of dissolution – all golds and russets and ambers in the dying light – level and streaked with dark waterways and the quiver and quaver of the muddy sands. Everywhere birds wheeled, seeking their night's shelter, scraps of white and brown and black against the tumbled confusion of orange sky.

The wind stretched in level swathes across the desolation, streaming low and keenly in from the west, bending the lissom reed stems in perfect unison, an undulating and unending suc-

23

cession of curtseys. Fox drew his old frieze coat about him, feeling his shoulders straining the frail material. He was growing out too big for the coat.

The smells of water and mud, of dampness and rotting vegetation followed them as the sun sank luridly beyond the turbulent clouds, horseheads of vapour boiling and prancing into the darker levels above. A light showed ahead from the square window of Uncle Ebeneezer's house, an upturned boat cosily furnished and warmed with driftwood fire. An upturned boat for home was a common enough sight, and Fox's first surprised reactions had long since passed with the year he had spent here. The ache of longing to see his family still persisted; but its keener pangs had dulled into a permanent sense of resignation.

His father had walked over four times to see him, and once his mother had come as well; but there was another baby and another on the way. To his pleas to return home they had replied, that soon, soon, he would come back, for his father was hoping to rent another room in the wooden house. But not yet.

Jake said: 'First thing tomorrow, Abe, we must go across to the gravel pits.'

At once Fox was back in the present, planning on collecting more ammunition.

'Aye, Jake. And this time I'm agonna get the roundest stones there is.'

Jake, rough and uncouth but with a great capacity for affection for this young nephew of his, a man with a twisted left arm that kept him free of the press, laughed.

'How many more times, Abe! A flat stone, like a pear-stone. Them's the best.'

The black keel of the boat lifted against the sky. The light beckoned. Fox had fitted in well here, with Uncle Ebeneezer, and his son Jake and daughter Susan and Susan's daughter, Mary. There was no father for Mary that Fox had ever seen or heard spoken of, and Mary herself, three years older than Fox, knew nothing of her paternity and had told Fox that her mother would not talk of it, and scolded her when she did. Susan Fox was still Susan Fox, and did not wear a wedding ring.

Fox liked Mary. For one thing, she bore the same name as his mother. That gave her an inestimable attraction in his eyes.

Outside the thick oak door of the boat-house and suspended

24

by a rope from a crude beam hung a copper pan of indeterminate origin. It was remarkably battered and buckled.

Jake said: 'Better ring the bell, Abe.'

Fox shook out his red and white check kerchief, the white now a mousey grey, selected the best of the stones in his pocket, slipped it into the loop of kerchief. He eyed the copper pan in the dusk. Red light reflected from it, like a star.

His swing and hurl and release were smooth enough and the stone struck the copper pan with a satisfying gong-note.

But Jake was not pleased.

'You just his th' rim, Abe! A bird've got away. Then, mayhap, you'd've starved this night.'

With the speed and precision of a striking snake Jake flung his stone from the black kerchief. The copper pan span and danced and rang with a note that rolled out over the marsh.

'Like that! See!'

Fox tried again, this time concentrating on slinging the stone and not on the rich juicy bird he would eat this night, and succeeded in reproducing that deep copper gong-note.

' 'At's better, young Abe.' Jake spoke a little grudgingly. He never missed, and he didn't see why this young rip of a nephew should miss, either.

Inside the upturned boat only the inward curving walls and the keel in the centre of the ceiling gave any indication that this house had once beat against the wind and sailed many a good load from London Bridge down and around the coast. The stone-built chimney smoked gently, and the fire blazed. Spring on the marshes was a time when fires were still a comfort.

'Dad back?' Jake asked Susan.

Susan was short, rotund, apple-cheeked and always busy, with a flour-streaked apron and a smudge upon her nose. Her hair was invisible beneath a mob-cap that Fox, for one, could never understand how it remained perched aloft. Such a gargantuan construction must by the laws of gravity themselves collapse into a great puddle of white cloth. But Susan walked with her little back-wiggling strut about the house and, lo and behold, the mob-cap never once fell.

Susan's daughter, Mary, sat at table darning a petticoat she had torn clambering about the marshes that afternoon. Her long naked legs stuck out from her black skirt. Her tongue stuck out firmly, and her eyes were screwed up in the flickering light. She did not look up as Jake and Fox entered. But Fox knew she was aware of his presence. He was nine years old; but his knowledge of the world had grown by leaps and bounds since he had met young Mary.

'Dad back?' Jake asked again, slinging the bird across.

'Not yet.' Susan felt the bird and smiled. 'You've still a good eye, Jake.'

'Ar.'

Uncle Ebeneezer had taken his catch in and from previous experience Fox guessed the old reprobate wouldn't show up until the morning. He'd roll in and groan and swear he'd never touch another drop of rum in his life – until the next time, the nine year old Fox knew with a worldly cynicism.

In the event he stayed away two nights and came aroaring in on the following morning, waving a rum bottle, his whiskery face aglow, and he and Jake at once started in on demolishing the bottle.

Susan shushed the children and gave them a heel of cheese and a crust of bread and sent them packing.

The singing and the roaring and the bedlam pursued Mary and Fox as they scrambled up the muddy bank on to the equally muddy track.

'We'd best not come back 'til dark,' said Mary, with a deep understanding of the weird ways of adults.

'Aye,' said Fox. His agile mind had fastened on one single objective in life, and this seemed to him as good an opportunity as he'd ever have. Apart from eating, which as an occupation took pride of place in his life, he was obsessed with Uncle Ebeneezer's punt-gun.

Many and many a time he had watched as the old man loaded the gun and fired it off, jumping at the bang, yet filled with a glorious sense of power and mysticism. Just to fire that gun off! Right from the moment he made sure the bore was clear until the moment he touched fire to the hole and leaped back! Just think!

Mary was game.

She hoicked her skirts up to her knees and followed him into the water. They climbed into the punt, giggling as it rocked beneath them. The sounds from the house drifted to them, snatches of song, roarings, the occasional smash as some object was dislodged from a shelf. Rum would cloak in oblivion all

26

the senses of those in the boat house.

Fox and Mary carefully poled the punt out.

The punt was in nowise remarkable a craft. Flat-bottomed, she sailed to Fox, already accustomed to the sharp-prowed wherries of the river, like a cow. But he manoeuvred her out into an open channel and sent her with the long and powerfully controlled poling movements he had quickly mastered on a dead straight course. Soon they were among the tall reeds, completely hidden. No sounds save the chuckle of water and the high screeching of the birds disturbed them. Mary's face, sweetly soft still with youth, with full red lips and eyes of so heavenly a blue that Fox could hardly remember anything else in all the world with just that gorgeous blue save the sky on a summer's day, smiled with mischievous excitement. Lord knew, there was precious little of fun in their young lives. Mischief like this was heaven-sent. It must be.

Fox knew exactly what to do.

He cleared the bore on the two-pounder. He measured powder. He rammed it down with a wad. He portioned out the scatter-shot, the right amount, wadded it and rammed that down. He primed the touchhole. Uncle Ebeneezer's tinder box struck after the first half-dozen tries and he blew gently. He caught the flame on the match and then looked up and gazed at Mary, leaning over him, her thin body taut in the ungainly black dress.

'What you waiting fer, Abe?'

He didn't know why he paused. There was some fleeting memory of being told about the punt-gun by his father; but he could not clearly remember just what it was his father had said. Anyway, the gun was loaded, the birds were waiting, Mary was with him, he was nine years old and a very devil.

He looked about for a likely gaggle of birds.

'Over there, Abe!'

Mary's voice screeched with excitement. She pointed with her left hand; but her right was fast clenched between her tiny breasts.

The day was bright and with the sun growing hotter as it pierced down through scattered cloud warm and pleasant. The birds wheeled and called. The gaggle Mary had pointed out had found something – a floating fish, a corpse, something – on the water, and were kicking up a ferocious din, calling and screeching and fluttering up and wheeling and diving back.

Fox edged the punt cautiously towards them, very conscious of the water and the mud and the tall reeds with their shining stems still and double with water-reflections. All his senses were alive and alert. This was a moment to cherish.

He moved the punt in the water, gently, pointed the flat bows at the gaggle of birds. The confusion over there was not interrupted by his movements. The gun's black barrel swung. He caught the punt's swing, held her, kept the muzzle of the two-pounder unerringly dead-centred on the gaggle.

'Go on, Abe!'

He lifted the match and blew.

Black and grey ashes charred and fell away. The tip of the match glowed red. He felt the kick of excitement through him.

Then he turned and thrust the match into Mary's hand.

'You wanna, Mary – I know. Go on!'

'Oh, Abe!'

But Mary was nothing loth.

With a sudden solemnity she thrust the match down on the grains of powder spilled around the touchhole.

The gun fired.

The concussion was marvellous, wonderful, glorious!

The punt surged backwards. The tongue of flame spat. The water roiled and the smoke billowed up, blindingly, casting a shadow down over them.

Fox could taste the smoke flat and bitter on his tongue.

The taste of powder smoke!

The shot was true. The pellets scythed into the birds. They screamed and soared and winged away and a great mass of them tumbled down, broken-winged, bloodied, to splash into the water like tears from the gods.

'Quick, Abe!'

The pole went in. The punt surged forward and through the choking cloud of smoke. They shot out and across the water, a dazzlement of ripples, glided in among the floating birds. Some still struggled in the water. Others floated, still and lifeless.

He and Mary began to pull them inboard.

They counted on their fingers.

'Twenty-four,' said Fox. Some little of his exaltation evaporated. 'Not so good.'

Loyally, Mary chided him. 'Two dozen is rare fine, Abe, for a first shot.'

'I got too close. The charge didn't have time to spread proper. Next time I'll wing three dozen, you see, Mary.' Then he paused. He had completely forgotten the clandestine nature of this operation. He looked at the birds stacked in the punt, and then at Mary, her hands in her lap, staring at him with shining eyes, those glorious blue eyes, her brown hair all atumble and ablowing in the wind.

'We'll put them into the shed,' Mary said with immediate practicality. 'They'll not notice.'

This was true. The three adults were still drinking, still roaring it up, happy on rum, oblivious to what went on outside. Mary and Fox were able to hang the birds in the lean-to shed beside the upturned boat, fasten the door, and then steal away. By the time the adults sobered up, they wouldn't know or care how the birds had got there. Uncle Ebeneezer would easily believe, with the evidence before his eyes, that he'd brought them in himself.

'Let's go see Chalky!' said Mary.

The stillness of the morning had given way to a breeze that strengthened, blowing Mary's hair, rippling the water which lapped close to the path. High tide mark normally lay below the path, but with the neap tides, or when wind and water coincided, the water would wash clear across knee high.

They hurried along towards Chalky's home, another of the upturned boats that dotted the marsh like weird primeval burial mounds. Chalky's boat was not as large as Uncle Ebeneezer's, but that did not worry the old ex-sailor as he lived alone, a true hermit of the marshes.

The path wended past an area of quicksand, and here Mary and Fox were very careful indeed not to stray. They eyed the unpleasant, sucking, slimy quicksand with great suspicion.

Used to wide flat horizons on the marshes which here and there might be broken by an upflung clump or an upturned boat, a wreck gradually subsiding into the mud or the straight bar of a raised road, the children were quick to spot the two horsemen from a good distance. They eyed the men on horseback with the lively curiosity of the young.

This whole area was a wilderness of mud, intercut by the winding arms of water and the treacherous patches of quicksand

and bog, open and scoured beneath the wind and the sky. Mary knew every inch for a goodly long way around home. Fox, too, had coped with the geography well enough not to get lost. Both he and Mary realised the two horsemen were lost, from their hesitant movements, no less than from their very presence here at all. They rode up slowly, clearly waiting for the children to reach them.

'Where lies the high road?' demanded the first.

Fox looked up in some surprise, scrutinising these two. They were both about fifteen or sixteen, beefy-faced young men, well made, robust. Their faces were very red. Their clothes were so fine they verged on the foppish, and Fox had never seen so profuse a display of lace before, not even in the beadle in his best. They were a breed of person with which he was totally unfamiliar.

The leader leaned down and struck Fox across the face with his crop.

'I said where away the high road, urchin! Answer your betters when they ask a question!'

Fox pointed, and found his tongue.

'That way.'

The crop lifted and lashed down again – but George Abercrombie was not caught twice. His face stung and yet felt numb. He had not cried out.

'You call your betters master, or sir!' The young man on the horse fairly snarled the words. His companion laughed and reined closer, the horses snuffling and pawing uneasily at the muddy ground. The two young men exchanged a few quick words.

Then they both dismounted.

They wore cloaks which they threw back with a great display of gallantry, an affectation quite lost on Fox, else he would have recognised their youth and their attempts upon the manners of manhood.

Mary had all this time stood quietly by.

Now the first horseman approached her and lifted her chin in a gloved hand. She did not flinch. She had a better idea than her cousin of how one should respond to treatment from the gentry of the land. She let her eyelids lower over her eyes, and thereby presented a ravishing picture to the two young men, for all that her cheeks were smudged with mud and her hair blew tousled and free, for mud could not hide the healthy blush of rose in those cheeks, the wildness of her hair conceal its exciting red-gold tints among the brown.

The two appraised her, and Mary, suddenly comprehending what they were thinking, gasped, and tried to twist away.

'Now, Simon, here's sport!' cried the first, and caught her around the waist, lifting her so that her naked feet kicked in the air.

'Right, Bruce! And I'm your man!' The second pushed up and began to feel Mary's slender body in a way that made Fox clench his fists and start forward.

'Hullo! The brat shows spirit!'

Fox cried out: 'Leave her alone!'

The two young cockscombs chuckled at that. 'Not likely,' said he called Bruce. 'You clear off, bratling, and leave gentlemen to their pleasures.'

Fox tried to kick Simon in the shins and Bruce lashed out backhanded. He smashed his hand across Fox's face, across the smarting weal left by the crop, knocked Fox headlong.

His feet left the ground and he toppled back, off the road, sprawling down over the bank. He felt the quicksand lap greedily up around his ankles and grasped frenziedly for a greasy clump of reeds as Mary screamed, and screamed again.

Chapter Four

The quicksand clutched at Fox, sucking him knee deep. He felt the greasy stems of the reeds slipping through his fingers, felt them cut his flesh. He pulled, and slipped and the quicksand gurgled and sucked and now he was down thigh deep.

Mary had stopped screaming.

She understood these things, and she knew that one day she would have to face this. She was almost thirteen, and her figure, although slight, was that of a woman. She stopped struggling as the youths ripped her skirt off. She felt the fear; but also she felt the fascination. It had to happen; why then not by a gentleman?

The quicksand nearly took Fox.

He clutched the reeds and gripped and by exerting all his strength managed to halt his downward progress and even manage a laborious inch upwards. Even at nine years old Fox possessed a strength surprising – yet, perhaps, not so surpr'sing given his tough and stocky figure, the breadth of his shoulders and the open-air life of labour and work he led. He hauled again and felt the loathsome grip of the quicksand slide and suck away in a gurgle. He dragged himself up on to the path and lay in the mud, panting, feeling his face burning with the double blows, his legs numbed and cold.

He saw what the one called Simon was doing, saw Mary with her naked legs flashing long reflections in the watery sunlight. He got to his feet, took out his knife, held it as Jake had shown him, and advanced.

Simon never knew what killed him.

The knife went in under his ribs, the point broke into his heart, and he departed this life incontinently.

Bruce, holding Mary, saw, and yelled, and started back, incoherent with disbelieving horror.

32

Him, Fox killed by a leaping blow of the knife through the belly, and then a second and a third stab, upwards.

Simon he had killed with speed and despatch, quickly and cleanly.

Bruce went squalling and screaming, spattering blood, messily.

Mary sat up, put her hands over her face, and screamed.

'It's all right, Mary.'

Fox held the knife, unsure what to do. In his thrashing death Bruce had spilled over the path and fallen into the quicksand. Nothing of him was now visible. Without a clear thought in his head, Fox then did something that later he regarded with the amused contempt of the hardened campaigner for the green amateur.

He put his foot against Simon's body and rolled him off the path into the quicksand.

The horses stood, snorting softly, moving their heads from side to side. Presently they walked away, finding the path, moving away across the marshes.

Mary's slender body shook with sobs.

Fox picked her skirt up and held it out.

'You'd best put this on again, Mary – '

'Yes.'

Fox experienced a profound sense of bafflement. For the two young men he had killed he cherished a warm hatred that would cheerfully have resurrected them so that he might slay them again. Mary put her skirt on. She smoothed it out, knocking off clotted mud. She did not look at Fox.

They began to walk along the path meandering through the marshes.

Presently Mary said: 'You killed them, Abe. You murdered them. You'll be topped – '

'Who's to know?'

'But they'll be looked for – ' Mary shook her head. She had felt the beginning of Simon and had steeled herself; and then, suddenly, Simon was a corpse. Some of his blood had spattered her thighs.

'People are lost in the marshes.' Fox didn't want to go the way of Uncle Abercrombie. He was a murderer. There was no gainsaying that. But what those two dead louts had been about merited death in Fox's young book.

Mary sensed this, and she did not venture any comments

about her own feelings.

When Fox said to her, a vague and puzzle alarm in his voice: 'You wouldn't tell on me, Mary?' she felt a quick anger, and then despair, and then determination.

So it was she could answer rationally: 'Of course not, Abe! What you take me for?'

'They deserved to die,' said the young Fox, and Mary was not going to betray that young belief, for she, too, was a Fox.

In after years, looking back, Fox could see no real reason to change his mind on that belief. What he would have done would have been to take what portable possessions the man had in his pockets, his watch, his money, his boots, his clothes, and sold them circumspectly. As it was, he supposed, at nine years old that was asking perhaps too much. The episode had been a shock for him. There was no gainsaying that. But he felt no remorse. None whatsoever. He knew nothing of the gentry, those who were the lords and masters of the land, save what he picked up in gossip; but if these two limbs of Satan were representative of the breed, then George Abercrombie Fox would always have a sharp knife ready for them.

Mary did say, a little venturesomely: 'Y'know, Abe. The fine folk think it's their privilege.'

'Not with you when I'm here, Mary.'

The gulf set between a nine year old boy and a thirteen year old girl is immense.

But Mary and Fox could find the bridge to span that abyss.

When he started to think back on what he had done he found a deep and thrilling sense of awe pervading him. He had killed his man! He had even remembered to wipe his knife blade clean on the dead man's clothes before kicking him into the mud.

Life was cheap in this day and age.

Thousands of children died every year from malnutrition; women faded into grey husks, shawl-clad, empty of hope or feeling; men sought work and slaved all the hours God sent for a pittance – and the fine lords and ladies and the gentry of the land lolled on their estates and in their fine London houses and grew richer and fatter on the proceeds of graft and corruption. All these things Fox was to discover as he grew older, and all lent weight to his estimation that he had acted correctly that day on the marshes.

They could not forget the incident; but their young minds

34

were resilient enough for them to be completely natural when they reached Chalky's upturned boathome. True, every now and then Mary would rub a hand down her stomach, absently, and Fox would glance at her and frown. But his knife, shining clean, snugged in its sheath over his hip, and he could give himself up to listening to Chalky's tales of the navy.

'Hullo, Commodore, come aboard!' hailed Chalky, waving his clay pipe at them from the doorway. He stamped his peg-leg in the length of timber serving as a step. An old man, this Chalky, so old in the young eyes of Fox that he might believe anything the ex-sailor might tell him. His bewhiskered face looked like the rear end of a chicken, bristling white hairs sprouting profusely everywhere. His eye was keen enough, though, and had he still had two he could not have seen more of what went on.

At the hail of commodore Fox relaxed. Had Chalky called him captain, he would have hauled his wind and stood off, and Mary would have understood.

'Drop your hook, young Abe.' Chalky puffed his pipe as Fox dropped down on to a coil of rope next to the barrel on which the peg-legged sailor sat like a figurehead. 'And you,' Chalky nodded to Mary. 'The Fair Sex is always awelcome.'

Chalky called Mary 'The Fair Sex' whether he called Fox commodore or captain. The commodore appelation, which meant fair weather, came from the noted Commodore Fox who in 1747 had captured forty-eight French merchant vessels – a total tonnage of 16,051 tons, and crews to the number of 1197 men, all taken prisoner – from the homeward-bound French West-India fleet off Cape Ortugal.

The captain naming of Fox was altogether different, when Chalky was in an ill-humour and wished to be left alone, and this came from the unfortunate Captain Fox who in the same year misunderstood signals made in the Battle off Finisterre in which Rear-Admiral Hawke scored a notable victory. Captain Fox was acquitted by court-martial of neglecting his duty; but was nonetheless dismissed his ship, the *Kent*.

'Did I tell you how Admiral Byng looked the morning they shot him?' asked Chalky reflectively. He sucked his pipe, which emitted only a wet glugging sound, and philosophically scraped it out over his wooden leg.

'Yes,' said Mary promptly. 'What about the lady who st wed away – ?

'Ar!' said Chalky, and laid a finger alongside his nose.

'Tell us about the *Foudroyant*, Chalky!' said Fox.

'*Foudroyant*? Ar! Capt'n Gardiner, it was, got a muskit ball clean through his head. Went in small, come out with the back of his head spraying like a dog diggin' a bone hole! Ar!'

Fox listened avidly.

Chalky had no time for officers with their gold lace; but he cherished sharper animosities for the petty officers of ships, for the bosun's mates, and the ship's corporals, and the master-at-arms, and for pursers he held an all-consuming contempt. 'Pussers,' he would say, "as been aput on this Earth to screw the blood from a 'onest sailorman's heart, and to charge 'im double for his 'ammick and his roundshot. Ar!'

The story of how *Monmouth* took *Foudroyant* was well known; but Fox listened screwed up into a kind of ecstasy, drinking in all the lurid details, in his imagination there on the deck in the powder smoke, reeling to the crash of the guns' recoil, shouting encouragement to the crews, pointing with a sword at the high banked 84, roaring his men on. Lieutenant Robert Carket had taken over when Captain Gardiner had been slain, and he had fought and won.

When the stirring tale was finished with the arrival of *Swiftsure*, Captain Stanhope, and the striking of *Foudroyant* when her captain, du Quesne, insisted on presenting his sword personally to Lieutenant Carket, in token that he it had been who had won the victory, Chalky said: 'It was a great and gallant vic'try, sure it was! *Foudroyant* had long forty-two pounders and twenty-four pounders; all we 'ad was twenty-four pounders on the lower deck an' twelve pounders on the main deck.'

'Yes,' said Fox, the blood drumming through his veins. 'An' the Frogs could fire off one thousand one hundred and thirty six pounds – an' we c'd only fire off five hundred and forty pounds!'

'Right old mess the old *Monmouth* was in, too, nigh the end.'

Chalky made no comment on Fox's complete remembrance of the figures, for although they were mere abstract figures they meant to Chalky remembered flame and smoke and the shattering smash of broadsides. Chalky and Mary were used

36

to Fox's phenomenal memory and his powers of mimicry. He had not really forgotten what his father had told him about Uncle Ebeneezer's punt-gun; he had simply chosen to push it away out of the forefront of his mind, and all this instinctively, without the need of thought.

A skein of geese passed over head and a badelyng of ducks began creating away and Chalky said: 'Whistle a few up, commodore, for supper.'

Obediently Fox pursed his lips and produced a faultless imitation. He clucked and chirruped away and presently was rewarded by a few birds winging in lazy circles.

'Which one, The Fair Sex, d'ye choose?' wheezed Chalky.

Mary pointed and in the instant of her finger straightening Fox let fly with his red and mousy-grey kerchief and sped the stone true. Another followed as soon as he could reload. Mary ran back, laughing, carrying the ducks dangling, one from each hand.

'You'll do, commodore,' chuckled Chalky.

'Et moi!'

They looked up as Etienne dashed across the mud towards them, whooping in excitement to be out and with his friends again. He hauled up in front of Chalky, panting, and said: 'I 'ave run all the way. Parbleu!' He broke into his own French heavily larded with French navalese, and full of oaths that would have horrified his mother. The Lamberts lived in a toppling wooden house over on the other side of Uncle Ebeneezer's upturned boat house, the father had married a French girl and her English was so atrocious as to be non-existent, so that Etienne her son and Therese, her daughter, spoke French better than they did English. The French was Norman French, as they were proud to boast, and Fox had picked it up with an ease that cost him no effort in the year he had known them. He was constantly amazed that Mary had so much difficulty speaking in French.

He and Etienne gabbled away, exchanging all their news – athough mention of two gentlemen-corpses did not enter the quick conversation. Mary and Chalky grew exasperated, and finally, with some deliberation, Mary kicked Fox. He sprang back, fists cocked, and Mary laughed. Etienne, too, laughed, and spluttered away in his English which was, in truth, quite as understandable as his father's.

37

Etienne, a year older than Fox, was no match for him in a fight, as their first encounter had quickly proved. Now they were friends, the four of them, Etienne and Therese, Mary and Fox, and they roamed the marshes, and called in at Chalky's, and in general were devils afloat or on the mud.

They asked after Therese, to be told her mother had insisted she stay at home at her needlework, whereat Mary frowned, for Therese, almost her own age, was a wonderful gossip. The Lamberts were an interesting family and Fox, at least, had no real idea what the father did to earn their living. Now they all set to to pluck the ducks, and bustle around, and so cook up a grand meal, half a duck each.

As the long sunset colours stained the marsh and mudflats in oranges and beiges, with vivid cobalt and indigo, emerald and black lowering opposite that outpouring of tempestuous colour, they bid Chalky goodnight – he had rattled on about the time he had led the boarders to take a French first rate and had expatiated on the plunder he had picked up in the great cabin, plunder all now, alas gone and spent – and then the three children set off home across the watery waste.

They bid goodnight to Etienne and watched until his trudging figure vanished in the shadows, and then they went into the upturned boat.

The three adults were all asleep, all asnoring, all dead drunk. More than one rum bottle lay on the floor, empty.

'The morning will be a right old roarer!' said Mary. She made a face.

They prepared for bed, and as Fox crawled into his cubby down in what had been the bows of the old boat, Mary put her head in past the torn gap in the curtain.

'Abe,' she said, and then paused. 'Abe – about – you know what. Thanks, Abe.'

She hurried away. It was too dark for Fox to see her face; but she had sounded as though she fought back tears.

Chapter Five

After his sister Susan's birth in 1768 the next yearly child, a boy, had died in infancy, and in 1770 Archie was born. The next child, a girl, called Mary, had lived with, it seemed, all the promise of her mother's beauty before her. But she, too, died in 1775, the year Fox spent on the marshes and he grieved for her with the sharp pang of personal loss. In 1773 a boy came along, Christened Ebeneezer, after a certain rapscallion of the same name. In 1774 Alfred was born and Fox returned, at last, to the old wooden house with its rented rooms to find him bawling lustily and his mother pregnant again, with, as it turned out, young Bert.

Coming home was a strange and daunting experience. The closeness of the hovel, the eternal dampness that struck him now quite differently from the muddy wet freshness of the upturned boat, the incessant yelling and bawling, the tears of the infants, the eternal scraping after a crust, made life so intolerable for him, despite all the love of his parents, that he craved for the free open sweep of the marshes once more.

His aunt, Elizabeth Lovett, tried to help in the bedlam; but she had turned out a pale, ineffectual, hand-wringing creature. It was left to his sister Susan to undertake tasks far too daunting and strenuous for any seven year old girl to tackle.

George Abercrombie Fox could see nothing clear ahead of him. He had been given this strange idea of thinking about his own personal future by Etienne's mother. Her strong practical Norman-French instincts for survival had braced up in Fox an idea that he ought to take thought for the future; and yet — every thought of the Foxes was bound up and enshrined in the glorious career as a carpenter brother John was to undertake. The money for his apprenticeship was laboriously scraped together, and hoarded, and gloated over, every mildewed penny and tarnished sixpence of it. This would bring security to the family. John would be their salvation. Everyone took quite for granted that one of their number would be placed in a situation where he might look forward to comparative affluence and would then automatically and without question undertake the care of the remainder.

That was what families were all about.

During the latter part of his stay on the marshes a fixed determination of his life had gradually changed. The single dominating influence on his thoughts, for as long as he could remember, had, of course, been his Uncle Abercrombie. George Abercrombie had always assumed, somewhere deep in the set of illusions about the world he carried about with him, that all in the fullness of time he, too, would be a highwayman.

Being a highwayman appeared the only way he could provide himself a pittance and his family a livelihood. He would be an honest highwayman, for his mother had been very strict in her injunctions of morality and honesty and sobriety. He had felt all the dark thrill of admiration for Uncle Abercrombie tempered by the conviction that his uncle must have been a bungler, or worse, to have been so stupidly caught. If he was to be a highwayman, then he'd damned well be a good highwayman. Like Robin Hood, he would take all the money and watches and silk kerchiefs and gold-knobbed canes from the rich people and give the proceeds to the poor.

Charity began at home.

But now, with old Chalky's wild tales, a new germ had entered his mind.

He had greeted brother John with wild whoops of delight and they had gone hunting Hogans.

John and the Fox allies had been going through lean times. The Hogans swaggered about, bullies, crowing over their victory. Outside the *Crown* where always were to be seen gin-sodden wrecks littering the gutter and the steps leading down to the waterfront, Fox espied a naval officer. He had probably dropped in for his dram after inspecting some detail on a ship on the stocks. His gold-laced hat winked in the sunlight. The autumn day, verging on to winter, really, had broken out with the last golden fling of sunlight anyone would see until the next Spring. Fox felt the old familiar marsh instincts aroused, a new skill against an old animus.

His red and mousey-grey kerchief was whipped from around his neck, a stone snatched up from the road fitted snugly in the loop – John cried out with a horrified yet exulting disbelief – and Fox let fly. The two boys were over a side wall and crouching among the warped timbers of a lumberyard as the officer's brave hat flew from his head, carrying with it his wig in a birdlike tumbling through the air.

The man let out a shriek and clapped a hand to his naked scalp.

George Abercrombie and John hugged themselves with glee, their brown eyes bright over the wall, full of a malicious young boy's humour.

'Anything that call itself a gennelman is fair game, Johnny.' Fox did not elaborate on that, and John was ripe for mischief, and for a short time the haunts around the *Crown* and the dingy street of wooden tumble-down houses nearby became notorious among the wearers of gold-laced hats.

When Fox and John, with their allies, Peter and Charlie and the Gibson boys, at last encountered the Hogans and their allies, the fight was long, blood-curdling, extraordinarily exhilarating and, beginning one-sidedly, ended most decidedly one-sidedly in the opposite direction.

Patrick, Shaun and Mick Hogan, with four of their mates, plus two dubious hangers on, quickly put out of the fracas, were supremely confident of victory. They started in on John and the Gibsons, Fox flung in Peter and Charlie, and when the cobbles were alive with the writhing forms of boys bloodily engaged, charged in himself with a bottle held high.

This was not a broken bottle and Fox's aim was to crack a few skulls, not to slice noses or blind. He brought the bottle down with satisfying cracks, he kicked with his horny toes into private crevices, he punched noses and eyes, and, in short, he let all know that George Abercrombie Fox was home again.

The Hogans fled, horse, foot, guns and baggage.

His father said that evening: 'Well, George, I hear you're home.'

And his mother said: 'Oh, George! Poor Mrs Hogan!'

John said, stoutly: 'Now I can run errands again, mother.'

So it was with much more of the feelings of a traitor that he cared to admit, Fox, the following spring, was once more packed off to Uncle Ebeneezer. Archie, now six years old, this time went with him. Young Bert had duly been born into the world, and Mary believed she was pregnant again. Seeing the fertility with which she bred, she took a complacent pride from the relative easiness of her childbeds – Mrs Hogan yelled and screamed and near kicked the place down each time.

Going back to the upturned boat and the marshes was, as he had not expected, a strange new experience. Perhaps young Archie, for whom Fox entertained a lively respect, had something to do with it. He cuffed Archie around the ear and said: 'Now you behave yourself, young Archie, you mind!'

Whereat Archie kicked him in the shins and ran off, and fell face down, smack into a stinking mudpool festooned with gas-emitting rotting vegetation. Fox hauled him out with a philosophical shrug; although the word would have meant nothing to him then.

Uncle Ebeneezer met them with a great laugh and a hug, and Susan baked an immense duck-pie, and they ate until they were stupid, and then both packed into the old three-cornered apartment in the bows of the upturned boat. Mary had been pleased to see Fox. She had smiled at him, and lowered her eyelids, and gone on with her work. Jake had clapped him on the back, and sized up Archie, and said: 'We'll have him knocking birds outta the air better nor you, Abe, afore long.'

They routed out Etienne and Therese Lambert, and called on Chalky, and Fox was again fired up by the old man's recollections of his days as a man-o'-war's man.

This summer ought to be a long golden wonderful period; and yet he felt the lack, the emptiness, he felt old before his time.

Archie fitted in well, despite a streak of rebelliousness in him that sometimes made Fox seem a reactionary. Archie was full of fire and spirit and anyone who tried to tell him what to do had to prove they meant what they said. His father had won his points by parental authority; Archie's comrades had to prove them by their fists. And Archie, at six, made no scruples where he kicked a fellow.

The first time Fox went swimming with Mary he noticed with an astonishment he could not fully understand that her tiny breasts were now much larger, with a shape, and that her body was no longer the thin and active body that might have belonged to a lad. She was almost fourteen. She was developing fast. For Mary the sight of Fox, with his chunky body and broad shoulders – and he only ten! – brought back vividly the day on the mudflats when Simon and Bruce had been killed. He liked her, there was no doubt of that. That was very clear.

She felt with the strongest of convictions that she could not tell him what she and Etienne had discovered this winter; but she felt strongly that she would like to share the discovery with Abe, and let him taste the delights too.

Fox was an apt pupil.

As the summer went by he found out much of the wherefores and whyfores of life, and, thereby became greatly enamoured of Mary. He developed quickly. And, all the time, the yarns that old Chalky span, chuckling and drawing on his clay pipe, and carefully scraping it out to save the last of the tobacco, and winking, and not seeing what was afoot between these two, made Fox more and more sure that what he had half-decided on would be best for the family.

Prize money.

'Ar!' said Chalky. 'When we took th' *Santy Bella* we all had gold to jingle in our pockets!'

Fox knew nothing of the outside world, and Chalky knew little more; he did know that men were talking of the colonies in America, and speaking with divided voices.

'They'll want ships now, lad, you'll see. If I was young agin, with me own spar instead o' this yere peg-leg, and two peepers, why, them Yankees is rich! Must be. Stands to reason. Don't pay taxes, do they? Well, then, what do they do with their gold? Hey?'

John Fox ought to find more permanent work in the dock-yards if what Chalky said was true. John Fox had a certificate of exemption and he cherished it as he cherished few items in his inventory.

'Steer clear o' the Press, commodore!' said Chalky. And he spoke in a voice grave and sober, and quite without the slightest suspicion of a chuckle. 'Best find a capt'n as'll give you a berth. They'm always wantin' fine upstanding young lads.' Chalky glanced at Mary, and chuckled, and sucked his pipe and said: 'Aye, fine upstanding lads'll always get on.'

With the strange and disturbing feeling of being a traitor, Fox found himself, one day when he had called for Etienne, discussing his future with Mrs Lambert. She was a sharp woman,

43

hard-headed in her Norman way, not beautiful but with ruddy good-health and a bold eye that clearly indicated why her husband had married her.

She and Fox carried on their conversation in rapid French.

'I have heard, young Abe, of a society who help boys who want to go to sea. There are more than one of them; but I believe M'sieur Jonas Hanway's is the best.' She laughed. 'He is the man who walked about with a little canvas roof over his head in the rain – '

Fox didn't believe that.

'The Marine Society, dear Abe, might help you. I think they started ten years ago, and as they are still running, that must prove they are respectable.'

Fox wasn't so sure. And anyway, how did one go about joining this Marine Society? And where was it? Mrs Lambert did not know; but supposed it to be somewhere in '*Londres!*'

'Find a good orficer and git a berth with him,' advised Uncle Ebeneezer later on.

'Steer clear o' that danged Press, though.'

'He's only ten, father!' said Susan, irritably. She was trying to sum up just what her daughter Mary was up to these days. The Good Lord knew, she didn't want another problem in the family like the last time – that had been Mary herself, poor mite! Best get this ferocious young Abe shipped out.

Uncle Ebeneezer ignored his daughter. 'That is if'n you want to jine the navy! More fool you, if'n you do.'

'But – ' said Fox. He looked up at this uncle of his, wondering how his Uncle Abercrombie would have looked and behaved, and wondering, too, just why he hadn't gone into the Navy or the Army in preference to taking up being a highwayman.

'It ain't all that bad, Dad!' snapped Susan.

'You don't know nuthin' gal, and don't you fergit it!' Uncle Ebeneezer was mightly restless tonight, having been without rum for three days and aiming to take his punt and his birds in in the morning. 'I ain't ahavin' young Abe here run off to jine the navy, God help him! without his father and his mother knowing.'

'You wouldn't stop me?'

Uncle Ebeneezer cackled. 'Stop you, young Abe Fox? Like as try to stop a runaway bull, as stop a Fox like you. I knows 'em. I knows the Foxes passing well. Once you gits your head down there's no stopping you.'

Archie caused a fracas involving a spilled bowl and a great thwacking with a spoon then, and no more was said by Uncle Ebeneezer before he left with his birds and his punt to sell them and buy rum – and supplies, if he remembered. Fox made up his mind.

He told Mary.

'I'll be sorry to see you go, Abe. Come out th' back. I've thought of something new we can try – maybe you'll git there this time.'

But Fox was only ten. He, too, was sorry to say goodbye to Mary – as to all the others on the marsh – but he fretted. If he and Mary had been nearer of an age, then, perhaps . . .

He walked back home alone, knowing the way, and at first he walked with his hand on his knife-hilt. After a time he took to cutting at the thistles along the road, and then he began whistling, and skipping, and running a space, and so with a sleep in a hedge, he reached home in the best of spirits.

After his parents' surprise at seeing him, he told them why he was back.

Mary shrieked and clasped him to her and John looked very grave. They were both unhappy. But, as Fox said: 'I'm doing no good at home, mother. And there's money in it. Chalky told me. Doubloons! Pieces of eight! Why, I could come home with a fortune!'

'Yes, dear George, you could.'

'That'll be the day, young 'un.'

Both knew they could not stop him. He'd just run off. Mary sighed. She looked at her husband. 'Is this what comes of going to Uncle Abe's execution, dearest? Of having this young rapscallion in the gutter?'

John Fox, in his turn, sighed.

'If Johnny was older, and apprenticed, we could look out for George. As it is – '

'You see!' said Fox, triumphantly. 'It'll all come right.'

Without parental opposition, with parental blessing but with a great deal of parental reluctance, George Abercrombie Fox set off to join the navy. He was accounted mad in some quarters, and in others was wished all the bed cess in the wide world –

this from the Hogans – and in others was regarded as no end of a devil. But no one envied him, except, perhaps, the next condemned criminal to step upon the scaffold.

And, perhaps, not even he, if he knew ..

Chapter Six

George Abercrombie Fox decided, not particularly rationally and not at all calmly, that he would first shoot the Master-at-Arms and cut off his head and boil it, would string up the cook and all the bosun's mates he could lay hands on, would in various gory and unbecoming ways dispose of most of the other petty officers, and then would set fire to the ship and dance about in glee as she burned to the water line and sank.

He wasn't much concerned about anyone at all – except Davy Lockyer – surviving. He rather felt that if anyone of the ship managed to escape what he had planned and swam ashore he would put his foot on their faces and shove them back and under.

George Abercrombie Fox, servant aboard *Henrietta*, it was clear, was not a happy boy aboard this King's ship.

He had been placed across the breech of one of the upper deck twelve-pounders, his trousers had been pulled down, and a rattan cane of extraordinary hardness and cutting stiffness and whippy springiness had laid across his buttocks. He had, without any concern over pride or dignity, yelled like hell.

He wouldn't sit down for a week, that was for sure.

He dragged himself off, after the surgeon had doctored his bottom with some foul-smelling gunk that might have been used to pay the lower hull and bottom of the ship herself, to his cranny between frames on the forepart of the gun deck, separated from the men. Being a Fox he would not, of course, descend to tears. But he felt his bile rising and the anger, and the misery, and the hopelessness of his lot.

And he'd chosen it himself, of course.

There had been no difficulty at all about joining the navy. He had grown used to ships when, from an early age, he had accompanied his father to the dockyards to see what work there

47

might be. The smell of ships, the sight of them, the feel of them in his mind, the shape and line and rake of ships, all these things he had been thoroughly familiar with from the earliest of his recollections. Now he was finding out what conditions inboard were like. He was not seasick, for which he showed no especial gratitude to a kind Providence but only the usual small-boy jeering taunts of those who heaved their guts up at every roll.

On that very first day he'd found young Davy Lockyer sprawling over a cable on the jetty and had hoicked him up with some cheerful small-boy insult. They had fought at once.

Lockyer was thirteen, a head taller than Fox; but Fox had jabbed a cruel and unfair knee into his belly and then hit him on the mouth and so struck him down. After that they had gone aboard and somehow, in the nature of things, they had grown close together as friends. Davy Lockyer, alone of the people aboard *Henrietta*, would keep his life when Fox at last set fire to the ship.

Fox had said he was thirteen, and the Purser had winked at him, and so written him down, and then had smudged the entry so that it was indecipherable.

'They'll sort you out when the time comes, boy.'

'Aye aye, sir.'

Henrietta was a sixty-four. Fox knew that. He knew, also, that she carried twenty-six twenty-four pounders on her lower deck, twenty-six twelve-pounders on her upper deck, for she had not been modernised, and six pounders on her forecastle and quarterdeck. Her complement should have been five hundred men; but, as usual, she was short of hands.

She was wet, dark, unaired, rotten, damp and mildewed and the men said her bottom would fall out at any moment.

During their passage out – Fox thought they were going to Americky, but no one seemed to be absolutely sure at first – the gun deck presented such a spectacle of vomit, excrement, filth and litter as to resemble a battlefield. Fox was as perfectly accustomed to unpleasant smells as any one else of his time; but he found the stench abominable. He also so thoroughly disliked the lack of air below that he would sleep on deck if he got the chance and some interfering ship's corporal did not thwack him with a rattan and send him packing below.

Davy Lockyer, who like Fox was not an apprentice, did

have a stroke of luck and got himself appointed as servant to one of the warrant officers, the Sailmaker. The Sailmaker, of course, was not one of the important Warrant Officers – the Gunner, the Boatswain or the Carpenter – but he did carry enough authority so that Lockyer was spared much of the hazing and bullying that all boys not specially appointed had to undergo.

Fox's main activities involved mucking out the manger, swabbing out the filth, the excreta, the straw, washing down and making clean. He was kicked by a cow's heel and carried the bruise all purply black for days. He was given all the most odoriferous and pestiferous and maladorous jobs that could be found. If he rebelled, he was laid face down over a gun and shown that rebellion, of any sort, was mutiny, by God!

'Lucky you wasn't shot, or strung up at the yard-arm,' said Bully Travis, servant to the Bosun.

Travis was fourteen, all ready to step into the glories of becoming a seaman, and he fancied himself as a tough. All the boys truckled to him. They had to. He had disciplined Fox the first day aboard; and Fox, fighting like a wildcat, had been knocked down, got up, been knocked down again, got up – and only no longer rose when he was jeered because he was unconscious.

At that, as some of the seamen said, for a young 'un, short and only ten – his real age was no secret – he had given Bully Travis a fight for his money.

Fox had no idea what the captain's name was – he supposed there was a captain aboard – and he never saw him, even when he made his rounds, for a seaman would shove Fox down some convenient hole, out of the way, getting rid of an eyesore.

Fox wore an old pair of trousers from slops, and a red shirt. For cold weather he had a frieze coat, and a black scarf, very thin and patched as to the corner. This scarf Fox set great store by.

Alongside Davy Lockyer, Fox sometimes thought he would place Mrs Thomson, who was stowed away with him down some unnoticeable cranny during inspections and rounds. She had given him an orange, and, later, had even parted with a little rum. Women, of course, were always great smugglers of liquor aboard, and although Fox had no idea how many women there were aboard *Henrietta*, Mrs Thomson was the only one who showed him any kindness. She belonged to the mess next to his own, and sometimes, thinking of Mary, he wondered how long it would be before he could press her to further kindnesses.

The routine of the ship which was strict and invariable he quickly came to understand and cope with. It was not this that made of his time aboard *Henrietta* an irksome period of his life. Much of his duty lay in helping the cook, a peg-legged man but otherwise sound. Fox had scarcely believed there were that many pans and buckets and kids in the world, or that elbow grease could bring up such a shine. But he learned

The beef, usually so hard it could be cut and carved like mahogany, was served out on Tuesdays and Saturdays, and the pork, little better in texture, on Sundays and Thursdays. The pease soup, which was generally reckoned to be the most palatable item of provided food, was not issued on Mondays, Tuesdays or Saturdays, and Fox, along with everyone else, developed surprising ways of spinning out the rations.

Any preferential treatment he might have expected from his position as scrubber-out of coppers to the cook vanished when Bully Travis hove up and said: 'Any duff comes your way, Fox, you 'ands it over. See!' He leered on Fox. 'An' I wanna see no teeth marks, you little toad!'

The round brown biscuits with their reefer's nut in the centre, which were edible only in the dark when the weevils were not visible at the beginning of the voyage for Fox – he rapidly overcame any scruples about eating, his small-boy stomach welcoming anything he cared to put into it – could be put into a bag and beaten until they formed a kind of flour. A little pork-fat and sugar added and the concoction baked, produced an acceptable duff. Occasionally, the cook would condescend to toss a morsel to Fox. Each mess aboard, usually of eight men, would contrive this kind of delicacy for itself, and Fox had thought himself well in, until Bully Travis hove up.

The head, a peculiarly revolting place, to which Fox would betake himself when he wished to go to the lavatory, was always an exposed position, wet and windy. There were two, one on either side of the bows, for the men and boys; the sick and the Warrant Officers might use the roundhouses, but little more comfortable.

One day, when he was thoroughly fed-up with Travis, and

through his malignity against the top-boy finding some of the spirit he might have lost, Fox discovered a gob of excreta upon the wood near his foot. There was nothing unusual in this and a bucket of water would have cleared it off, a job for which he usually was first in line. Now, however, he carefully preserved the nauseous lump. When the cook gave him a piece of duff, with a gruff comment: ' 'ere, nipper, wrap your guts aroun' this,' Fox made his usual thanks and took himself off.

He passed Davy Lockyer, looking very white-faced and pinched about the eyes. Lockyer was one of those who was undergoing voluntary constipation rather than face the horror of the head. Unusually, Fox avoided his friend.

His knife – that noble instrument – had never before descended to such ignoble work; but, nevertheless, Fox did it. So, carefully and without a hand-tremble, he cut a slit across the chunk of duff, opened it out, scooped a hollow, dumped in the excrement, his face struggling between its usual frozen look of detached hauteur cloaking misery and a strange and new glee, closed the lid down and smoothed the sides round to cover the slit.

The scooped out stuff he swallowed down with gratification. Then he let Travis find him and bully him out of the duff.

George Abercrombie Fox made sure he was around when Travis, off in a corner between frames with his cronies, bit hugely into the duff.

For Fox the ecstasy of actually being himself again, of doing something that swam directly against the tide, was as intoxicating as the rum he now drank with as much panache as the oldest shellback afloat. Although well-watered – three-part rum was acceptable – it still gave him the strange and eerie sensations he recognised must be incipient drunkenness.

Now he hugged himself, seeing the world again in new colours, waiting the reaction of Bully Travis.

Bully Travis roared into the boys' area aswearing and ablaspheming. He kicked Davy Lockyer out of his way. His face, bloated and engorged and quite unlike that of any normal fourteen year old boy, loomed in the low tween-decks like a violent sunset over the marshes. The boys scrambled out of his way. He carried a colt, a rope's end, and he swung it hissing in a narrow circle.

His face was unusually clean, and particularly in the area

around his lips looked well-scrubbed.

Fox laughed.

He stepped forward and he laughed.

'Enjoy your duff, Travis?'

Travis' high whine choked in his throat with his anger. He lunged forward.

'I'll cripple you, so help me!'

The rope's end thwacked around. Fox ducked and felt the hemp smash agonisingly down across his shoulders. Travis drew back for another blow, clearly aiming for Fox's face. Fox drew in a deep breath. He knew he was no match for the bully; already he had been smashed to the deck in a fight – a fight he had fought with his fists – so now was the time to fight as Fox would usually fight.

He kicked Travis in the genitals.

He kicked hard, he kicked with passion, he kicked with an unholy joy.

Travis stood upright, the rope's end still whirling for what seemed to the waiting Fox a long time. His face turned various colours from its high red. His eyes bulged. He opened his mouth but he could not shriek. He was rigid. Then he was limp. He fell, awkwardly, twisting on the deck. His head struck the cascabel of the twenty-four pounder and he choked something, a tremble fluttered all his limbs, then he collapsed like a flung-down sack of meal.

'You've killed him, Foxey!'

'Travis! Bully Travis, down!'

Fox bent, grasped the boy's shirt collar, hauled him up.

'He ain't dead,' said Fox. He felt the most profound disappointment. 'It's lucky for him he ain't.' He glared at Ginger Spry, a toadying crony of Bully Travis's. 'When he comes around, Ginger, you tell him. You tell him good. I could've kilt him, now, just like that – and if he comes agin me again – if he touches me again – I will kill him.'

Some of the boys were murmuring and already the seaman charged with their behaviour was beginning to think he ought to look at the outcome of the fight.

'You remember that, Ginger, and tell 'im, the little toad.'

Fox could recognise the disappointment now. He had been keyed up for a fight, a good rousing hell-roarer, and the fool had struck his head against a cascabel and knocked himself out. He saw clearly the fight had been merely postponed.

And, too, he heard himself speaking, and recognised how he was breaking a cardinal rule.

Never promise to do something to someone – just do it.

Jake had said that. Jake with his twisted left arm, who could defend himself with the best.

Jake and the marshes, his parents and home, seemed a long long way away right now.

But he had struck a blow for his own personal freedom.

He knew, quite simply, that if Bully Travis created any more trouble he would kill him. Aye – and without remorse afterwards.

George Abercrombie Fox recognised the lice of this world when he saw them and if his remedy was rough and unmerciful – that was how he had been trained.

Chapter Seven

The extremely tall and broad-shouldered man with the great mop of flaxen hair, the man called Swede, said he was sure they were sailing north into cold waters. He added, with a smile that came easily to him, that, by damn! that was better than sweating it out in the West Indies.

He was from a fishing village up in Scandinavia, and by calling him Swede the men showed no disrespect whatsoever; rather, it was a mark of affection for a good messmate.

Like most of them, he had been pressed off a merchant ship, and with an adaptability had settled down into a first rate able seaman. With him, Fox found much to his surprise that he was striking up the friendly relationship that had to exist between a prime seaman and a boy if the boy was to learn the ways of the sea and himself turn out a sailorman.

Davy Lockyer, as a servant, might easily miss a great deal of this essential early training. The life was greatly more difficult for Fox; but Fox was being knocked, hammered, forged, driven, into the mould of a prime seaman. At the time he felt like striking back at every watch; but he did not – at least, not against Swede – and he learned quickly.

There was much to learn.

Everything aboard had a name. A seaman must know every name, what it meant, and where it was kept. He must be able to rush on deck and select, for example, the fore-topgallant starboard brace, without fail, in the blackest of nights and in the most tempestuous of seas, with the sleet slashing across his face and the cutting spray driving into his eyes, his hands blue and numb and bending like three-inch iron.

Fox learned.

Henrietta might be an old worn-out tub of a little sixty-four; but she carried three masts and yards, a bowsprit, she carried guns, she carried pumps and magazines, powder and shot rooms, and filling rooms, she had a hold crammed with barrels, and bilges that stank to the trucks, she had gangways and companionways and ladders and rope-ladders – and in principle she was exactly the same as a first rate of a hundred guns and three decks and an Admiral in a gold-laced coat.

What he learned here would stand him in good stead all his life and it was his good fortune, to which at the time he was blind, to fall into the hands of Swede who was a prime seaman who knew every single trick of his trade there was to know.

During an engagement his duty would be to carry powder to the guns, and he would, initially at any rate, be responsible for supplying one gun only. The gun assigned as his was a twelve-pounder on the upper deck under the gangway in the waist – one to starboard and the corresponding gun to larboard.

'If'n we's engaged on both sides, young Fox,' said Swede, who was the gun captain, in his respectable sea English, 'Slushy'll skipper second gun and yo'll sure have to run double-quick time, eh?'

The gun second captain was responsible for handling the opposite side gun in the event, which was unusual, of the ship being engaged to starboard and to larboard simultaneously.

So Fox had to learn his way from the blanket screens where the men handed up the charges in their wood and leather containers, up the ladders and along the deck to the gun. Then he must return by a route that did not conflict with those boys ascending, a kind of circular route. He had to be as agile as a monkey.

He was not watched and so rated as an idler; but there were no idle hands aboard a King's ship.

During this time – where they were Fox had no idea at all – Davy Lockyer grew more wan and peaky until even Fox began to worry.

Lockyer was forced to go to the heads by the Master-at-Arms, a certain Mr Doherty.

This man was God-Almighty's god-almighty deputy, as far as the men and boys were concerned. He carried with him an aura of dark and harsh authority, of absolute dominance and terror. Boys would turn and run if he hove in view.

A large man, Mr Doherty, with that leather-grained skin common among sea-faring men, yet with Mr Doherty the greenish cast to that tough skin lent a sinister aspect not lost on the men and boys of the ship. He had stringy red hair, and eyes that stared perhaps too fixedly upon the men. Fox had noted with particular interest the length and profusion of the man's red hairs within his nostrils. Mr Doherty as the Master-at-Arms was a man to whom the very widest berth possible should be given.

' 'An I'm to be servant to Mr Doherty!' Davy Lockyer said to Fox as the ship lay over to a strong westerly, driving north on the larboard tack. They had picked up sails over the horizon and lost them again; but the actual evolutions of the ship meant little to Fox at this time for all his world was contained within her wooden walls.

'Him!' said Fox, aghast. 'What about Timmy?'

'Mr Doherty's turned him out and disrated him into the manger lads again. I'm to – I'm –'

'Here, Davy, don't take on so! Maybe he ain't as bad as all that.'

'But – you don't know, Abe.' Davy Lockyer was the only soul aboard to call Fox by his second name, Abe. 'Why d'ye think he made me go to the heads?'

'Oh – no – ' Fox felt the abrupt smash of passion he could not identify or control and he gripped his fists so hard together his blunted, broken, blackened, split nails actually dug into his flesh. 'You poor bastard!'

Fox knew, as well as anyone else on board, that this was all a part and parcel of life for a ship's boy. No one had attempted him yet, presumably because he was, as the men said, so unsavoury-looking a morsel of boy. Lockyer, by contrast, was almost girlish-looking in feature and his curls did not help, either.

By this time the beer had become stinking and a pint of wine a day was issued. A boy was entitled to half a man's rum ration, issued as grog, and with all the cunning methods so well known to Jack Tar, Fox was able to make a little business of his grog, so that now he poured a sippers for Lockyer and told him to drink up quick and stop blubbering and think on about what best to do.

Many of the ship's company were mad.

Fox could see even with his limited experience that men did not normally do the things these men did as a matter of course.

No one bothered. Provided a hand did his duty and did as he was told then he was tolerated. Madness, Fox soon discovered, was congenital in the navy, a condition to be lived with, and not to be afeared of if it struck him down. He did not mean to go mad, for he was already formulating a system of behaviour, a crude code of conduct, that would lead him on, he believed, to his true goals in life.

Davy Lockyer went from bad to worse and there was nothing Fox could see that he could do about it.

'It hurts so!' Lockyer said, and blubbered, at which Fox gave him a gulpers of rum and banged him across the shoulders in wordless boyish sympathy.

His daily tuition under Swede proceeded when he had done the tasks for which he was responsible. *Henrietta* had fallen in with a little squadron – some of the men claimed to recognise the ships in company and called out their names – and some great scheme was afoot. Swede's pigtail was not particularly long, and privately he told Fox that he had no time for these great waist-length hanks of hair.

'But they guard your napper from a cutlass, Swede, don't they?'

'Nah. They might, happen the cutless swung slow-like. But, Foxey, my boy, when a cutlass you swing, you swing it hard and heavy, ja?'

'Ja,' said Fox, dutifully.

The major work of *Henrietta* at this time had been in support of the land forces and almost all her marines had gone ashore as well as a number of seamen with the guns. To his intense chagrin Fox was not selected to go ashore, and had, as he said, to damn-well rot at anchor while the others had all the fun. There was always work to do, and the news was scanty and unreliable. In truth, all his horizons were bound up within the ship herself. He heard the name of the admiral who had taken over command – Lord Howe – and he gathered that the navy was unsuccessfuly attempting to blockade the coasts, for the American privateers were many, fast, daring and creating havoc among British shipping.

Mad keen as he was to see some action, he also wanted to go ashore, and for the crew to return and for them to set sail. Anything would be better than this.

Davy Lockyer was in terrible straits at this time, but Fox

knew there was nothing he could do. Mr Doherty caused a young ordinary seaman, a youth from Wapping who should have known better than to be caught by the press, to be given a taste of the cat. Fox watched the flogging with the fascinated gaze of a rabbit watching a snake, as he thought of it, only too well aware that when he grew up he would find himself strapped to the gratings and the flesh being stripped off his back.

He was always cuffed about the head when given an order. This was a normal part of life and something he could learn to live with, always providing he had the chance to duck and dodge and so evade the major force of the blow. And yet, not all the men cuffed him about. Swede, for instance, got into a real humdinger of a scrap with Big Ben, a Liverpool man with a sour temper, when he caught him maltreating Fox.

Big Ben roared and struck out and Swede ducked and struck Big Ben in the stomach.

That was the end of the fight.

As Swede said, afterwards: 'Big Ben haf a rupture as big as my fist. Hah!'

So many of the men suffered hernias that it was a mere part of routine.

The problem of Bully Travis had been partly solved as he had gone off with the landing party.

But Davy Lockyer was continually in trouble with Mr Doherty, and Fox saw his friend grow paler and more finely-drawn day by day.

In all honesty and with all the clarity of vision of which he was then possessed, Fox couldn't see what to do. He was only too well aware that he was a younker. His eleventh birthday came and went during his time aboard *Henrietta* and by the mocking smallness of the number served to remind him more strongly that he had a long way to go before he was a man, before he could think of knocking the Master-at-Arms' head off with his fists. During this period in American waters many incidents occurred to Fox and he passed through scrape after scrape which in after life he would recollect, with humour, with scorn, with awe at his stupid intrepidity – but never, he hoped, with shame.

He did manage a few runs ashore, mostly to collect water and firewood and help with driving the cattle that might be brought down to the shore, or contriving to herd along the squawking feather-fluttering chickens; but in general his life remained strictly within the ship. He was fascinated by the country, seeing in the immense stands of timber, the distant prospect of blue mountains, the flash of white to indicate a cabin snugged in the greenwood, a life so far distant from his own back in London that how the two could co-exist in the same world puzzled him.

New York which he felt to be an inferior imitation of London did not interest him as much as the fervent idea of the great open spaces. Men were deserting all the time and running, to trek out into the wilds, fighting animals and Indians, fighting Yankee or Briton, fighting anyone and anything that might cross their path. Now, if he was to run – running was the dream of most men and certainly of all those pressed into the service.

But, if he ran, what of his chances of prize money for his family? He had signed on for money. A boy received no pay, and so far the rebels had not come flocking up to hand him their gold, as Chalky had suggested they would.

During the period in New York harbour the ship was attacked by a crazy American in a boat that swam beneath the water. Fox heard all about it from Swede, who had it from a marine who because he had suffered a fractured arm – happily it had mended for him tidily – had been left aboard and did solitary sentry duty before the aft quarters.

'Damned Yankees!' said the marine. 'What'll they think of next! It be agin nature, that's right! A boat, swimming *under* the water!'

'I don't believe it!' said Fox, with youthful certainty.

'If Harry, here, heard the orficers talking about it, my little Stockholm-tarred bratling, Foxey, then it be so, ja!'

'But how?'

Harry the marine rubbed his arm with an old gesture. 'I did 'ere the first lootenant say as 'ow they'd heard 'twas a fellow called Bush something, a right maniac, by all accounts.'

Later Fox heard about *Turtle* invented by David Bushnell which had, with, of all things, an army sergeant called Ezra Lee aboard at the controls, wallowed under the water to attack *Eagle*, the flagship. Fox, suddenly, with a shiver he remembered again at a later date, imagined what it must have been like. How brave could a man be, he often wondered? He had not yet been

59

in action and the craving to pit his own courage against the horrors he knew awaited him gnawed at him.

Ezra Lee must have been a giant among men to have done what he did. If the Yankees produced men like that – men who were really Englishmen – and Scots and Welsh and Irish, too – then this war might be longer than the general expectation.

And, supposing Fox was called upon to kill a man like Sergeant Lee, a quondam Briton? Somehow, doing a mischief to a man you knew and who had done you down was a simple matter compared with this cold-blooded animosity against a brave man defending his own country – although they were a pack of rebellious colonists, really, refusing to pay taxes, so it was said, to pay for the war against the French that had secured their own country for them, at the cost of British blood and British gold.

Despite this growing awareness of horizons outside those of *Henrietta* and with them a consequent wider understanding of just what he, George Abercrombie Fox, was doing here, three thousand miles from home, his main and continual preoccupations lay within the ship. A new captain was appointed, and Fox heard his name – Captain Shotter – and with him a new slew of young gentlemen and servants and midshipmen.

Fox detested midshipmen.

All the Lower Deck detested midshipmen.

They weren't seamen, they knew nothing, but they were gentlemen and officers and as such must be treated with the same cringing fear and respect as any other officer.

And, by God! how they abused their authority!

Fox felt all the futile rage boiling and seething in him as men with whom he was by now building some ties of comradeship were strung up at the gratings and flogged all on the lying word of an adolescent midshipman.

To the ship's boys the midshipmen were merciless.

Absolute and implicit obedience to the slightest order was required of the men and whilst, although bitterly and with many a curse, they would obey the officers whom they knew understood sea duty, for the immature midshipmen who ordered and struck and got them the cat they had a deep and abiding contempt. Fox became the particular butt of Mr Midshipman Lafferty. This young gentleman went out of his way to make life miserable for Fox, and although as a boy he was not flogged, yet the boatswain caned him across a gun so many times on the word of the insufferable Lafferty that Fox now entered one of the blackest and bleakest periods of his life.

Because of this unwelcome downturn in his fortunes, Fox became less aware of Davy Lockyer's sufferings. Mr Doherty, the Master-at-Arms, pervaded a chill of horror wherever he went, and some of the men, idly pursuing the age-old pastime down in the forward hold of matching fighting rats, were caught out.

Every one was flogged, unmercifully, viciously, so that their backs swelled and burst and the blood spattered. Fox with the hands was forced to witness this. He felt no revulsion at the sight of the blood and at what the flogging was doing to the backs of the men, he was used to sights like that; but he felt two predominant emotions. One was scorn for the men that they had been caught matching rats. The second was a fierce and corroding hatred of all authority.

It was not fair; but justice and fair-play had no place in George Abercrombie Fox's life.

He afterwards believed that it must have been during this period that he began, and dimly, to see that if there was to be any future for him – and as a consequence for the family of Foxes by the Thames – he would have to claw himself out of the pit and instead of being on the receiving end of the cat all in due time, so contrive it that he was the one ordering the cat to be administered.

He, G. A. Fox, would be the one to wear a gold-laced hat and wear a sword and carry a telescope under his arm. He would stand on the quarterdeck and look down, safely ensconced behind a file of blank-faced scarlet-coated marines, and watch as a seaman's back was sliced to ribbons.

Yes! Better that than being the seaman triced to the gratings!

Ambition was born in Fox.

His acute mind and prodigious memory would stand him in good stead. That mind, however, tended to fudge the outlines of his true motives. His responsibility to his family was minimal at this time, and he understood that, because Johnny was to be a carpenter and earn a good wage and the family would thereby be raised out of the abyss of poverty. So he could not in all truth say that this dark and secret ambition grew in him through responsibility. It grew and strove upward from the dark of the Lower Deck to the light of the Quarterdeck because Fox wished fervently not to be flogged, wished not to suffer the pain and humiliations of the Forecastle, wished to have decent food in his belly. The idea of wearing good clothes was important; but weighed nothing against the power of flogging, conditions and food.

So, wrapped in his own misery and in his grandiose, nebulous – impossible, almost – dreams, he failed to see just how tragically the day to day grind was affecting Davy Lockyer.

Davy came down into the boys' space in the tween decks crying, his face streaked with the greasy-grey marks of his tears. He did not sit down.

'That bos'n,' he said, choking. 'Mr Doherty tells him to lay it on extra hard for me, Abe. He does, I knows it!'

'The war'll soon be over, Davy. Then we can go home.'

'Naw. It won't. There's never goin' to be an end to this. That's what I knows!'

Fox tried with a few rough and awkward words to comfort his friend. But he was already looking forward and dreading his next task, for that toad Mr Midshipman Lafferty would be standing on a gun and superintending, with a sneer and a string of curses and a cuff around the head. And if Fox dared to lift his eyes it would be Silent Insubordination and the bosun's cane. It would be that, anyway, since the midshipman would eventually find some pretext or other to have Fox punished.

'I can't stand it any more, Abe. I can't!'

'It's rough, Davy. My oath! I know that!'

Fox was no longer thrust into a hiding place during rounds and was filling out and adding a few inches to his height, which was never to be great, and so Davy Lockyer could say meaningfully and with sense: 'He'll be after you soon, Abe.'

Fox pushed that away, thinking of the slug Mr Midshipman Lafferty. Any complaints would be met with an instant reprisal, for a midshipman was a gentleman and therefore his word was sacred, and Fox had heard the captain say that he meant to see every manjack aboard understand that a midshipman was an officer. Fox had early, on the marsh, formed an opinion of gentlemen. So he did not pay overmuch attention to Davy Lockyer's worries and fears.

For this he reproached himself afterwards.

He was learning never to look back, never to feel remorse, never to apologise and never to feel guilt over an action taken.

They were hard lessons; but they kept him afloat.

But over Davy Lockyer he felt all these heart-tearing emotions.

For Davy Lockyer went missing and *Henrietta* with her full complement was at sea, and there was only one place Davy Lockyer could have gone. Fox looked overside at the grey sea swirling past.

Poor Davy had thrown himself overboard.

To get away from his misery and Mr Doherty he had jumped and now the sharks were tearing his limbs from him and the fish were eating his eyes and gnawing on his flesh.

Chapter Eight

Davy Lockyer's name would receive alongside it the ominous initials: 'D.D.' Discharged Dead.

The loss of a ship's boy overboard was of no great consequence. The chief sufferers would be his fellow boys, for if he had happened to be servant to an officer that worthy would merely select a replacement. It was on the shoulders of the other boys that any extra work fell.

Henrietta hauled her wind south, with the eastern seaboard of America just over the horizon rim on the westward. Every one aboard was well aware that although ordered to keep a lookout for the daring American privateers that swarmed on the seas and took their toll of honest British shipping, the old sixty four even if she spied any would never catch those fleet hulls with their spread of canvas.

Swede had said: 'We're off an excursion, lads, I'd wager my grog on it.'

A new air of excitement permeated the old ship. No one laughed or even smiled, of course, in the presence of an officer. That was silent insubordination and could result in a red-checked shirt at the gangway.

The night was moonless but in the glitter of the stars and the glimmer of the sea the masts and yards, the swell of the canvas, all the rigging and tackle, stood out in bold black outline. *Henrietta* heeled gently, southward bound on the starboard tack, and, just as Davy Lockyer has prophesied, Mr Doherty sent for Fox.

Fox had been leaning out over the timber heads of the forecastle watching the run and curl of the water as it thrashed past, losing its creaminess in the glimmer of the sea and the darkness back there. He had just visited the heads, in this calm sea a relatively easy business, and was now going to get

Plan to enjoy life when you retire

Make sure you'll have the money you need with a little wise financial planning now.

GT. BRITAIN, CHANNEL ISLANDS OR N. IRELAND

BUSINESS REPLY SERVICE
LICENCE No. K.E. 1511

The Chief General Manager
THE PRUDENTIAL ASSURANCE CO. LTD.

142 HOLBORN BARS
LONDON EC1N 2NH

POSTAGE
WILL BE
PAID BY
LICENSEE

his head down. But, for a moment, he paused. Back in the wake the sharks would be following. In some of their bellies would be digesting pieces of Davy Lockyer.

Fox's face did not betray an iota of his feelings.

Already that graven iron mask had been forged to cover his ugly face.

Doherty's skin reminded Fox of shark skin.

Young Alfie Trotter, it was, who sidled up to Fox and with a smirk that the night and the absence of officers allowed, said: 'Foxey! Mr Doherty wants you. He said for you to cut and run and lively now!'

Fox didn't even bother to put a fist into Alfie's guts as he pushed past. His iron mask of a face betrayed nothing.

About the ship the orderly routine of night watches would go on. The sandglass would turn every half hour. The bell would ring. The lookouts would fight against sleep and the watches would change. On a night as calm as this there was even the chance that the hands might not be called on deck to change the trim of the canvas although, the first lieutenant and the captain being what they were, they might order all hands on deck just for the hell of it.

No weather can be trusted, however, and by the time Mr Doherty had finished with George Abercrombie, the ship was heaving and wallowing and the white-caps were roiling in from the north west, appearing like phantom horsemen from the circle of darkness about the ship and bearing up and down and corkscrewing her and tearing on and away on the opposite side.

Fox cowered out of the way as the hands boiled on deck to take in canvas, to get *Henrietta* snugged under double-reefed topsails. The gale worked up. By morning the sky glowered down a grey and charcoal whirlpool of massed clouds, the sun was invisible, and intermittent sheets of rain fell, scourging across the decks. The seams of the old ship worked and water seeped through, oakum fell away and caulking crumbled, so that the carpenter and his mates were constantly busy assisting the caulker in his duties.

Fox had no time to feel anything.

He took his turn at whatever duties he was called upon to perform. Somehow he found himself both wishing and despairing of the ship's foundering. He knew just one thing, at this time, and one thing only. That was the last time with Doherty. Never again. No matter what happened – never again.

The gundeck became a quagmire of filth again. Going to the heads was all but an impossibility in this weather and after Peter Jenkins, a prime seaman from Cardiff, had been swept overboard as he tried to relieve himself, the men simply used whatever convenient utensil was to hand and emptied it over-side. As it was, what with the vomit from those whose stomachs had not so far accustomed them to gales, the gun deck resembled a shambles. There was blood – Johnny Gumbo, a strapping Negro from Barbados, smashed his arm and head as the ship lurched and smashed him against the deckhead.

The gale seemed a minor event to Fox.

The violence as lightning shattered the sky in giant peals of thunder left him indifferent. He found himself urging *Henrietta* on into wilder and wilder movements. If she went on her beam ends and turned turtle, he would roar against the elements and, perhaps, laugh. He joined a line of boys passing up pannikins and kids and buckets of water, hurling it splashing overboard, with the wind, working until every single muscle of his body was strained past any rational breaking point – and still going work-ing on.

The ship did not sink.

Battered, spray-swept, she fought out the gale and came through.

Then there was incessant work until she was back to her pre-gale state. She had lost a yard and the fore-topmast and the carpenter and the boatswain looked glum as the jury-masts were fished. Everyone had been keyed up for the expedition ashore; this gale might mean they had lost their chance.

Excited though Fox would ordinarily have been by the promise of an expedition ashore, he was preoccupied and completely bound up with his own problems. In addition to the ill-treatment and abuse which he had to endure daily, he was now beset by the attentions of Doherty. He had no formulated plans. The power of a boy aboard a King's ship was near enough zero as to make no difference.

All he did know was that he would not endure Doherty any longer.

Once had been once too often.

Doherty was strong. He was immensely strong, as he would

needs be, being possibly the most hated man aboard.

Fox was to discover that not all Masters-at-Arms and Ship's Corporals were thus hated. Much depended on the temper of the individual holding that position, and on the way he carried out his duties. Doherty loved the power he held and the punishments he could bring for the slightest infringement of discipline. The smallest article left lying on the decks would bring its owner before the captain to be sentenced to be flogged; if the offender through fear of the consequences failed to claim the item then it was forfeited and auctioned off with the possessions of dead men.

To add to Fox's problem Bully Travis was back aboard, filled with lurid details of his adventures. The gale had for the moment prevented anything other than ensuring the old *Henrietta* still swam. So that Fox had pushed the problem of Travis away to fumble and fume and finagle a plan – any plan – in his young and distraught mind.

He had made a few friends aboard now, notably Swede who was a tower of strength, and William Loampitt, generally known as Sniffy Billy because he always seemed to have a cold. Also there was a growing number of the boys who had come to regard Fox with much greater favour after his adventure with the primed duff and the subsequent dealings with Bully Travis. Fox had, in a desultory way, gathered the beginnings of a gang about him; now he set himself assiduously by means of depriving himself of his grog to winning them over to his side. Already, although he was not consciously aware of its processes, that charisma he possessed was working away for him.

'Bully Travis reckons he's goin' to do yer, Abe,' said Joey. Joey was servant to the Master, and was therefore in something of a privileged position. He was thirteen, a good bright lad, and Fox nodded and said: 'He may boast, Joey; I knocked him down afore, this time I'll break his neck.'

Joey eyed Fox with some respect. Clearly, he not only believed Fox meant what he said, he believed that Fox could do just that.

In the aftermath of the gale and with the ship rigged all ship-shape and Bristol fashion again, Fox could get on with the problems nagging him. He knew Doherty would start on him again this night, when he had made his rounds, and Fox who did not make the mistake of failing to do what was required of him in the way of duty and cleaning of the Master-at-Arms' gear, suddenly vowed, a quick, intemperate, blasphemous promise, that if Doherty started on he'd do for him.

The decision came swiftly, out of the blue, into a skull empty one moment, and filled with a deadly intent the next.

'Tell Travis from me,' he said to Joey. 'One wrong step and I'll have his tripes for breakfast. See?'

Fox found the items he went looking for, loose scraps left in the armourer's cubby, stolen without a qualm. He hefted them in his palm. He nodded.

Like everyone else on the Lower Deck, he was on the lookout for white mice.

The latest positive information had added to the list of known white mice the name of one Samuel Rawlinson, a red-eyed man with thinning hair and a weakness in the same direction as that of the Master-at-Arms himself. As informers and spies, white mice were likely to find themselves suddenly the unexpected possessors of black eyes or broken limbs, or worse, if the hands became irked enough by their treachery.

Fox walked carefully. He had by this time perfectly accustomed himself to shipboard conditions, and could penetrate the most secret recesses of the ship without trepidation or hesitation. Mrs Thomson continued aboard and still with the same mess. Fox had discovered a better hiding place than the one she normally occupied and she had given him rum in gratitude. That rum had gone to swell the faith and loyalty in him shown by his fellow boys. He had also discovered by this time that there were fourteen women aboard, all discreet, their existences known but tolerated if they were not conspicuous at divisions or rounds.

With the lumps of jagged iron concealed in his pocket Fox returned, after evening muster, to his hammock space. He knew, this being the first tranquil night after the gale, he must expect Doherty to send a minion to rout him out. So he went up on deck and to the heads. Here, despite the desperate nature of the place, he could often be alone for a relatively long period. He kept a watchful eye on the larboard roundhouse for this was the one used by the Midshipmen and the Mates – and by the Warrant Officers. That on the starboard was used by the sick. He saw the nightly procession come and go, and waited while the hands saw to their needs, passing the odd jocular word or two when, for instance, a wave gave a man a wetting. Then, for a space, he was alone. As on that previous night calmness descended, despite the full-functioning of the sixty-four and her near five hundred men, everything was so well-organised, as it must be, that events could follow one another with a metronomic regularity.

Presently he saw Mr Doherty.

The man loomed gigantic in the night. There was now a rind of moon.

'Fox! Is that you, you young bastard! C'mere, you hairy awkward ape! I want you!'

Fox did not reply.

Enraged, Doherty climbed down off the forecastle past the knightheads and on to the beakhead itself. Fox moved silently and swiftly aside, clambered up the beakhead bulkhead. He moved cautiously and yet with supreme confidence. Doherty saved his breath for cursing in a low ominous monotone, and for climbing.

Fox looked back.

Doherty stood up, looking about, expecting to see Fox on the heads.

George Abercrombie Fox took off his black kerchief, looped it as Jake had shown him back on the Thames side marshes, carefully placed a jagged lump of iron filched from the armourer within that deadly sling. His face was no softer than the iron.

He whirled the sling, took aim, swung, hurled, let fly.

In the next instant he was aware of the starboard round-house and of the black bulk of a man emerging.

He saw Doherty fling up his arms. He saw the Master-at-Arms topple over. He hoped the man would fall and break an arm or leg on the hard timbers beneath. But Doherty tried to save himself, and by lurching sideways grasp the open rail. He lurched and grasped; but his clutching fingers missed their grip and he pitched overside.

As he went Fox thought: 'And good riddance to filth.' But he shouted, high and powerfully in his young voice: 'Look out!' And then, as the man from the roundhouse swung about: 'Man overboard! Man overboard!'

But, everyone knew, if you fell overboard in these waters your legs and your guts and your head would be devoured by the ever hungry sharks.

When an inquiry was held, Fox was able to say with complete truth that he had seen Mr Doherty fall overside. The man who had been in the roundhouse, a man whose word would be instantly accepted, had been the Bosun. He guessed that poor Mr Doherty had been taken short, had had not time to wait and had gone to the heads instead. It happened. He had fallen overboard. That happened.

The captain, to whom Fox had taken an instant dislike, praised the boy for his attempt to save his master, Mr Doherty, and commiserated with him that this had been unsuccessful.

All in all, so Fox considered, there could not be anyone aboard who could know – however much they might guess – what part he had played in this unfortunate tragedy.

So it was that when Bully Travis, and Ginger and one or two others, came looking for trouble, Fox picked up the belaying pin handy, and faced them without flinching.

He felt exalted, tensed up, confident that he could move mountains, if he had to.

'You touch me, Travis, and I'll bash your head in.'

Travis hesitated. This was a new Fox. Joey and one or two of the boys who remained loyal to Fox backed him up.

There might have been an impasse, had not Travis, conscious that this would mean a complete loss of face, pushed in with an ugly sneer and with a swift kick at Fox's groin.

'I'll git you, Fox! I'll pulverise you!'

Fox wasted no breath on words.

He caught the foot, twisted it, yanked and as Travis crashed past brought the belaying pin down on the boy's head. He missed his mark as Travis flinched, and broke the lad's nose. Bright blood gushed forth. Travis screamed.

Fox hit him again and then, as Travis fell, kicked him in the groin. He kicked him again as he lay on the deck, for good measure.

Then he faced Travis's cronies.

'I told you I'd half-murder Travis. Look at the toad! Anybody else want the same?'

There were no takers.

Later, when Travis, duly washed, presented himself for the surgeon's dubious inspection, he carried a tale of falling down and hurting his nose. The surgeon had to believe this, for it was so common an occurrence as not to be worth logging.

Fox found that his charisma worked; and, too, that the boys now no longer regarded Travis with the same fear. Fox wondered if they regarded him with fear. He found he didn't care. Just so long as they left him in peace.

He would go on working his fiddles, little devices that when he was a seaman, perhaps a boatswain, would develop into the wide-spread cap-a-bar practices that deprived the Admiralty of thousands of pounds worth of gear every year.

Then he reconsidered.

No – he wasn't going to be like all the other lads and dream either of going home or becoming a seaman, a warrant officer. He was going to be a real officer. A wardroom officer. Being a captain, inconceivable though it really was, might not, might just possibly not, be beyond his dreams.

Anyway, he'd started.

He'd go on in the same way.

Chapter Nine

George Abercrombie Fox felt the thick sweat starting out all over his body, the feel of the hemp ropes abrasive between his gripping fists and over his naked shoulder. His feet thrust at the dirt, he leaned into the pull, heaving for all he was worth as the struggling line of men wavered and heaved and grunted with a combined mutual effort to get the twelve-pounder on its clumsy carriage up the long slope.

All about Fox the visible presence of the American North east brooded on him, the vast forests of hickory and ash, of oak, elm and maple, forming a background unlike anything he had ever experienced before. The sky hung remote and whitely blue above him and the summer sun beat down harshly, bringing flies and midges and the nervous extraction of every ounce of energy in him to bear on the day's efforts.

Heave, you bastards! Heave! Lively now!

The boatswain ran along the line of toiling men, his rattan going like a fiddler's elbow. His mates with their colts also belaboured the hands. With a grunting heave the twelve-pounder surged forward again and this time, with a run and a rush, they brought it inside the wooden stockade.

Dust rose chokingly. The wood seemed to exude heat. For a moment the hands were excused to find themselves a drink and Fox slaked his thirst with water that had been drawn from the well, water that was fresh and pure and cool, so unlike the green-algae scummed gunk they were forced to drink aboard. When a sailorman ever drank water, that was, which was seldom if he could avoid it.

Fox was by now nearing his thirteenth birthday and although he had grown a few inches in height he remained short. His growth showed in the spread of his shoulders and the depth of his chest. He could feel his strength coming on him. Because of

72

that as much as his self-won position as a boy who would tolerate no nonsense from his equals – the taming of Bully Travis had become in the course of events common property – and was quick and responsive to orders, he had been selected to accompany the naval landing force as a messenger. The quick and responsive obedience to orders was all part of the Fox master-plan that envisaged his eventual wearing of a gold-laced hat.

The French were now causing more trouble for England with the rebellious colonists and Fox had heard many times that his messmates would love to drub those damned Froggies unmercifully, where there was a profound if seldom-voiced and inchoate reluctance to fight those same rebellious colonials.

Fox was illiterate as were ninety nine percent of his messmates; but here and there a man could read and write and Fox had listened as, most surreptitiously and with the utmost caution, the colonials' declaration had been read. To George Abercrombie it made fine stirring reading, bold words declaring ideals that he had not comprehended before. The great phrases put into hard form vague ideas that had stirred him. He felt that here was a line in which he could whole-heartedly believe.

'We hold these truths to be self-evident, that all men are created equal; that they are endowed by their Creator with certain unalienable rights; that among these are life, liberty and the pursuit of happiness.'

Well, that was clearly not so aboard a King's ship, despite that a few men had clawed their way aft through the hawsehole and trodden the quarterdeck. The truths were not self-evident. Men were not created equal. And there were no rights whatsoever unless you stood up and fought for them. George Abercrombie Fox, young as he was, had learned that the hard way.

But the hope and expectancy danced vibrantly before him and lured him on. He hadn't run yet. But he would run, as soon as a favourable opportunity offered.

And – damn the Indians!

If he couldn't reach a white colonial before the Indians scalped him he wasn't the nipper Fox, regarded with the deepest suspicion by the warrant officers and with some grudging awe and respect by his peers, and regarded as a mere mop-end to run and obey orders by the officers. It was all in the point of view.

The first lieutenant roared obscene words and the bosun repeated them, with fine floral additions, and the hands tailed on to the drag ropes again and once more the twelve-pounder inched laboriously forward. *Henrietta*, small and ancient as she was, was still as a sixty-four a valuable and powerful unit of the navy in these waters off the coasts, and she had gone in for as good a refit away from an English dockyard as could be contrived. In the meantime the seamen were occupied in dragging artillery out to the army forts. The war was not going well for Britain, what with Gentleman Johnny's surrender and the entry of the French. The Delaware line was collapsing. The Continental Army was proving a powerful instrument and although the redcoats could always win a battle, they could not as yet face the tactics devised by the rebels. Fox did not share the general humorous contempt for redcoats exhibited by sailors although open to all the suggestions of the navy, and he stubbornly stuck out in his opinion through sheer stubborn pig-headedness. Fox did not believe in trusting anyone he didn't know; as he knew few people he trusted practically no one; at the same time, young as he was, he wouldn't condemn the sojers until he had personally been confronted with their stupidity.

It went without saying that he hated all redcoat officers; they were of a kind with the naval officers, except they seemed more empty-headed, more aristocratic and more inhuman. Fox even felt sorry for the redcoats.

The sun beat down as they toiled through the forest. They dragged the artillery and canister and grape and the powder, massive and heavy weights, lagging stubbornly against the pull of muscles hardened by hauling at sea. The sun moved across the sky and a little wind got up and whiffled the tops of the trees. Birds flew; but Fox was too engrossed in throwing all his weight against the drag-ropes and having to pay them the attention he would have liked.

Every individual gun had its own individual weight, brought about through differences in manufacture; this particular twelve pounder weighed thirty-three hundredweight, three pounds, three ounces and three pennyweights – a plethora of three that amused Fox, in his lucid moments. Most of the time he was like them all slightly mad with the lunatic strain of pulling, of anticipation of an arrow or a musket ball from the forest, and of passionate desire for a drink.

The first lieutenant cantered back along the line of guns. He and the captain had been provided with horses. Everyone else, even the surgeon, walked.

The shadows drew down and the trees grew a more sombre shade.

'Step lively there, lads!' roared the first lieutenant.

The bosun reinforced that exhortation by fruity words and his rattan.

The bosun's mates added their quota of blasphemy and their quota of blows.

A section of light infantry detached from the light company preceded the naval landing party, and these men created a great impression on Fox. He knew that after the lessons learned in the French wars in which Canada had been gained the British light infantry corps had been disbanded and the rebels had taken up this mode of fighting again first. Now, however, the British light troops were once again proving their superiority. The Fifth Foot and the light and grenadier companies from eight regiments had won a decisive victory over the French on Saint Lucia. Fox took every opportunity to converse with the light bobs and to learn from them.

Of the Indians he had seen – Iroquois family, for he had not yet formed the quick appraisal of individual tribes although he knew the Oneidas were fighting mainly for the rebels – he was impressed, and fascinated. He admired their tanned deerskins and their moccasins and their fur robes of rabbit and bear skins. He felt amusement at the way they shaved their hair up both sides of their heads, leaving a cockscomb in front; but he was sombrely aware of the significance of the dangling scalplock at the back.

All these fresh experiences worked together in Fox. He found something new to delight him every day. And yet – and yet there remained the plague of Mr Midshipman Lafferty. If Fox had won through to some kind of recognition from his mess mates and suspicious acceptance by the petty officers, he was still simply an obnoxious ship's boy to the midshipmen.

With the sinking of the sun the light infantry reported that Fort Tarkas was in sight and their orders called for them to report back. Heaving at his drag rope Fox saw the light bobs melt back along the trail. The captain rode up on his horse towards the wooden palisade of the fort. Smoke rose from chimneys and cooking fires within the stockade. The Union Flag waved overhead. A redcoat shone above the wooden gateway.

The long evening light lay across the scene and Fox looked forward with the utmost desire to a rest and to the evening grog.

The log-gate opened and the sailors hauled their guns through.

Not a single thing, not a laugh, a snigger, a musket out of line, betrayed the trap.

Only when the sailors had thankfully hauled their guns into line and neatly flemished down the drag-ropes and were standing up and knuckling their backs and looking about for good spots, were the absence of redcoats and the appearance of tall and healthy-looking men in tanned deer-skins borne in on them.

But then it was too late.

Ranked muskets overbore them.

Captain Shotter, dragged off his horse, protested loudly; but a pistol shoved under his aristocratic nose quietened him.

Swede said: 'By jings! Yankees! All captured we are!'

'Rebels! Yankees!' The shouts of the sailors died away.

Fort Tarkas had been tricked into defeat. The small army garrison were penned in an angle of the stockade and now the naval contingent, also, were thrust in with them. Officers and men mingled, although the ranks separated out within the wooden walls, and the reason for this even Fox could see. There were precious few Americans who had carried out this audacious and successful coup. They had Indians with them – Oneidas, probably, although Fox wouldn't as yet know a Saulteaux or Metoac from a Piankashaw or Passamaquoddy. There were three major families, the Algonkin, the Muskhogean and the Iroquois, that Fox knew about. Every single one of 'em, he had been told, would scalp him and roast his heart on the pow-wow fire and have him for burgoo.

Of the old Five Nations he also knew, the Mohawk, Oneida, Onondaga, Cayuga and Seneca. Unless an Indian wore some clearly identifiable symbol of British loyalty, Fox would run and know he was no coward for running. Dead men would never collect prize money, that was for sure.

As a mere ship's boy Fox existed at the very bottom of the ladder. He had not even put a foot upon the first rung. So it was that he would never be consulted, never asked to give an opinion, never have his interests weighed in the scales of convenience and expediency. But he could be given orders.

The rebels handed out rations and water and the men ate. The bitter outcry when their grog was not forthcoming brought Indians crowding around the inner palisaded wall, facing on to the centre of the fort. The Indians looked as though the slightest excuse would serve for the beginning of a massacre and the American colonel after a few hot words with Captain Shotter and the army officer commanding, a lieutenant with a face like a sea-sick horse, managed to persuade them to quieten the men down. Fox fingered his hair. It was a dark and bushy mop kept reasonably clean because he hated the feeling of lice upon his body and in his hair although having to suffer them. Perhaps the Indians would save him the trouble of worrying about his hair.

The old Five Nations had become the Six Nations with the addition of the Tuskarora. Fox could imagine what warfare had been like before the treaties were agreed. His hair floated remarkably freely upon his scalp. He noticed that a number of his messmates had developed a nervous habit of stroking down their pigtails. He felt absolutely convinced that the Indians eyed those queues with a lively professional interest.

Very little of the food was wasted to be thrown on the sculch heaps. Jimmy Ducks came over and looked mournfully down on the rubbish and swill.

'C'd use that, right enough,' he said in his thick country burr.

Fox, who had received many a casual cuff from Jimmy Ducks, the slow-witted seaman in charge of the livestock, made no answer. He was more concerned with the seemingly lunatic activity going on in the centre of the prisoners' compound.

Although it was now dark torches had been lit and in their intermittent illumination a gaggle of midshipmen were larking about, wrestling and shouting and falling about. The toad Lafferty, as Fox saw with savage contempt, was prominent in this mindless activity.

Fox found himself a corner against rough bark and curled

up and got his head down. It seemed only moments later that the bosun was shaking him awake.

'Silence, boy!'

Fox remained mute.

'D'you come along o' me, younker.'

Obediently, Fox rose, stretching and rubbing his eyes. He followed the bosun through the darkness. Where the midshipmen had been larking the torchlight showed only their scuff marks in the dirt. He heard the clink of weapons beyond the nearside wall and knew the rebels were on watch.

'Down here, nipper, and keep quiet!'

With the casual cuff of the sailorman to help him on Fox stumbled forward out of the illumination and found himself among a group of officers. They turned their faces to stare at him. Those faces were white and exhausted, black-smudged beneath the eyes. Fox guessed they had not slept.

'This 'ere's the smallest on 'em, sir,' reported the bosun.

Captain Shotter stared in distaste upon Fox.

'He is short, bos'n. Can he run?'

'With me at his backside, sir, he'll run.'

'But you will not be at his backside, will you?'

'No, sir. Beg pardon, sir.'

A tenseness and a nervousness about these men communicated apprehension. Fox swallowed and glared down at his feet.

Midshipman Lafferty appeared. He was stripped to the waist and his shoulders, arms and back were rubbed red raw.

'It's no good, sir.'

Shotter waved a hand.

'Thank you, Mr Lafferty. If the Good Lord sees fit to endow you with shoulders, who are we to condemn you for that?'

Fox understood now.

'Do you remember the trail back to Fort Nahan, boy?'

Fox looked up and spoke directly to the captain.

'Aye, sir. I do.'

'Ha harrum! Then you will run back down that trail, and warn Fort Nahan. Tell them what has happened here. They will arrange our relief and rescue. Understood?'

'Aye aye, sir.'

A single word flew into Fox's head like a bright rocket.

Indians!

He was given instructions to which he listened in silence. They showed him the gap in the outer log stockade they had made, working, as he now realised, under cover of the skylarking of the midshipmen. The thick logs had been moved apart as far as they would go, until the earth and stone filling prevented further movement and no amount of shovelling would improve. It seemed that only the smallest of the ship's boys could squirm and wriggle his way through. In other circumstances Fox might have gleed at the discomfiture of the glory-seeking officers – that their rescue had to be trusted to the scruffy little half-starved and well-beaten ship's boy.

'You'll go whilst it's still dark and get clear before daybreak. Go as fast as you can.' Shotter wiped his forehead. 'I don't like the look of those damned Indians.'

That was what Swede had said to Sniffy Billy. None of the sailors liked the look of the Indians and all feared that the Americans would not be able to control their redskinned allies.

'Had he ought not to take a pistol, sir?' asked the first lieutenant.

Captain Shotter frowned.

'No. He must avoid noise. Now, boy, get along with you.'

Fox approached the wedge-shaped crevice between logs.

A bulky man in a soldier's red coat and with the insignia of a sergeant major appeared. His face, as hard as a loggerhead, seamed and brown, showed now an expression that at first Fox did not recognise. Then he understood that this flinty soldier was expressing concern and sympathy and a better understanding of what was being asked of this scruffy ship's boy.

' 'ere, lad. Rub this on your shoulders.' Fox took the grease and smeared it over himself. The sergeant major held out a pair of moccasins. 'These'll be better than your feet, lad. They're quiet, like Indians. Put 'em on.' Fox did so. They were pliant deerskin, soft and comfortable. They felt good.

Without any fuss, without a clap on the shoulder, without fanfare, George Abercrombie Fox squeezed through the gap. He felt a horny hand on his bottom thrusting and then like a cork from a bottle, he popped through. He reached back to check his knife still snugged over his hip. Then, quietly, he crept away from the fort and disappeared into the shadowed woods.

Chapter Ten

If they thought he – George Abercrombie Fox, who had the honour to be named for his uncle hanged at Tyburn – was meekly going to run off to Fort Nahan just to rescue a gang of gold-laced soft-handed toffee-nosed officers, they must be crazy!

This was his chance to run.

He'd find some Yankees and tell them he wanted to join up.

He'd quote their Declaration of Independence at them and say he believed he was entitled to a share of all that loot; they'd give him a musket – a rifle, if he was lucky – and a coonskin cap and he'd go off happily shooting redcoats.

'Shot the redcoats in the road, Scalped 'em neat and handy! Going back to scalp some more! Yankee Doodle Dandy!'

That sounded the life for George Abercrombie Fox.

He knew the kind of rifle he wanted, not the Canadian type shooting balls of thirty to the pound, but the American frontiersman's type, shooting balls of sixty to a pound. Yessirree! He'd show these damned toadying officers what was what.

It would be stupid to go back to Fort Tarkas.

So he padded on along the trail, watching the leaves dark against the sky, listening for the first crack of a twig, the first sound to betray he was being followed. He knew the reputation the Indians enjoyed of silent movement; but he felt sure his quick young ears would hear them. After that he'd have to hide – and hope. He did not want to run across any Indians, thank you.

Fox was moving well in America.

The trail presented no difficulties and he padded along with his head rotating like an oast house vane in changeable winds. He was slow to realise that fatigue and excitement and the

80

constant apprehension of Indians were working on him with subtle power, making him almost – almost but not quite – lightheaded. His thoughts which at first had jangled in his mind were now slowing and lengthening and he did not look back so often.

The moon cast a greenish tinted silver across the trees and the rocks of the trail. He heard a wild animal call, a cry which choked off immediatey. The wind moved stealthily. Shadows were darker now, against the moonshine.

Just ahead, past a turn of the trail around a prominent stand of timber, lay Fort Nahan. He remembered dragging the guns through on their way to Fort Tarkas. He padded on.

Now he passed through the worst period of tiredness. He wanted to lie down on the grass and sleep. A short sleep would refresh him. But he dare not delay. The Americans might lose control of their Indian allies before long and after that there would be bloody work at Fort Tarkas. He had to get the relief party alerted and moving out fast.

The shock of realising where his thoughts had led him pulled him up, so that he teetered with one leg grotesquely in the air.

Wasn't he going to run? Then why was he so concerned to reach Fort Nahan and rouse the alarm?

Surely – surely he should simply lie down now and rest and then push on in the morning, avoid the fort and get back to the Yankees along the coast. The rebels would welcome him, of that there was no doubt. Then why was he pushing on towards the fort now?

Swede was back there, and Sniffy Billy. They were mess mates. Fox had no real friends, and yet – and yet. How would he feel if Swede had that yellow hair yanked off his scalp, all bleeding and hideous?

Swede?

No – he would have to raise the alarm. Once that was done he could think about running.

Where the trail passed the end of that projecting tongue of trees the woodland had been cut back and the trail ran for a space between rocks. He remembered the immense effort called from the men to drag the guns past here.

The fort lay ahead and no lights showed. Well, that made sense, he supposed. The Yankee marksmen were notorious.

The night smell of the woods faded a little. The moon

brightened. As he approached the fort he kept vigilantly alert, somehow, because he was George Abercrombie Fox, not rushing forward and whooping and hollering. He went forward warily.

He heard the first screams when he was some two hundred paces from the main gate.

He was still dog-tired; but as there was something now to do then tiredness could not be allowed to hamper him. This was a lesson the Navy had hammered into him the hard way, and which he had bitterly resented. It had taken Swede with his wisdom of many years at sea to teach him that when a thing must be done then the only way to do it is to do it, never mind what conditions or pains interfered. Those screams meant the fort had been taken, for they were not the cries of any ordinary pain, as from a drunken brawl. He covered the remaining ground to the main gate at top speed. The shadow of the bulky logs fell across him and then he was inside the open gate and huddling in the deepest of the shadows within.

The man was completely naked. He hung upside down from a wooden triangle and the three Indians were just beginning their devotions to his bravery.

Very little in life had power to sicken Fox, even at twelve years old, nearly thirteen, and so he was able to look on and plan and not spew his guts out.

As he stood watching he first loosened the knife in its sheath and then he unfolded his black kerchief.

No thoughts other than a fierce and dominating drive to save the white man from the redskins occurred to him. He admired the Indians for their courage and their woodcraft and their stamina, and he had even an inkling that torture to them was administered as a mark of respect to a foeman. But that was not Fox's way. To him, an Englishman, torture was anathema.

The first stone hit the first Indian on the temple and he dropped silently. The other two were slow to react, to Fox's surprise, and even as they yelled savagely and looked about, he dropped the second redskin with a stone between the eyes.

The third, unable to spot his assailant in the shadows, fled. He made a poor target in the moonlight and Fox did not waste slinging time. The Indian dived into the shadows beneath the catwalk around the parapet. Fox did not move. If that Indian was a marsh bird, now, then Fox knew how to stalk him. That he was not a marsh bird but a powerful savage armed with a tomahawk and a knife meant only that Fox must take thought for his own safety. But the principles of stalking remained.

Now he could take notice of the dead redcoat, his head a festering black in the moonlight, sprawled by the gate. Beyond him lay other men, seamen and soldiers, all scalped. In the harsh moonlight their shapes lay like a twisted and devastated moonscape, black and silver, deathly quiet.

Not a one had a musket or bayonet, not a one still had his ammunition pouch or a knife. It was stone and sling against tomahawk, then. Carefully, Fox moved sideways beneath the parapet's shadow. He did not make a sound. He did not hear the Indian; but he knew the redskin would be stalking him, too.

The naked upside down man on the torture triangle had stopped that initial wracking screaming; but he continued to moan in a bubbling groaning. Fox had to ignore that, to force it out of his awareness the better to concentrate on listening for the Indian.

A thin clatter broke from the shadows to his left. He stopped at once and remained still. That had been a pebble, striking wood. If the Indian couldn't do better than that ...

By keeping his breathing controlled into a smooth and easy rate, by a conscious flattening out of body-processes he thought he was just about as noiseless as he could ever be. He moved forward like a ghost. The redskin had vanished into the shadows beneath the parapet. Initially, then, he had been something like ten yards away. He had thrown the pebble and Fox had not heard the throwing, only the striking.

That might be the way of it if the savage got him in his sights. There would be no sound, and then the tomahawk or the knife would bury its deadly metal in his back.

With a mental curse as blasphemous and filthy as any the Lower Deck might use, Fox forced that kind of thought away from his mind. Ten yards. Closing. The shadows beneath the catwalk were inky. The silver moonlight flooding the central area with its flagpole and its tortured man lay thick and brilliant by contrast. The bodies of the slain lay here and there, where they had been killed and dragged for scalping. Again Fox had to drive from his mind the idea that there might be more than just these three redskins left to amuse themselves with the last

white man; drive the idea away but nevertheless keep it somewhere at the back of his head for future emergencies.

The odd idea had just occurred to him to wonder how some
aristocratic midshipman would handle this situation when
another clatter sounded. This time it came from ahead, between
him and his adversary. Fox did not smile. He seldom had anything in his life to raise a smile. But, now, might be the time
for a smile. The redskin was getting worried.

He couldn't see a damn thing in these shadows.

But then, neither could the Indian.

Carefully, soundlessly, one moccasined foot after the other,
Fox edged his way along. A pair of thin, gaitered legs stuck
out into the moonlight. The boy's body lay in shadow. Close up
to him Fox could just make out the brave uniform, and the
outflung arms, the hideous black blotch that was the drummer-
boy's head. Fox had had his eye on him. Now, moving with
a delicacy of touch as light as that of a butterfly, he felt past
the head, hoping he would not be disappointed, and his groping
fingers touched the smooth painted wood of the drum.

An arrow had feathered itself through the skin, cutting it
cleanly. A black stain lay across the drum, black and sticky
yet, blood. One of the boy's hands still grasped the leather
strap. Fox began to pry the hand loose. Rigor mortis had not
yet set in fully and he was able to move the fingers, one by
one, lifting the dead hands from the instrument that had
brought the boy out here to the American wilderness and his
death. The little finger was reluctant. Fox felt that if he used
force and broke it the little crack would be picked up by the
redskin's ears, and if he sawed it off with his knife that, too,
would betray him.

Silently, he wrestled with a dead boy's little finger.

All the time he was mentally counting off the time. If the
savage had moved forward at approximately the same rate as
himself, he could not now be more than a few feet away.
Absolute blackness lowered ahead, cut by the silver bar of the
moonlight. No shadow would betray the Indian. At last Fox
prised the little finger free. He held the drum suddenly thankful
that the arrow had taken its voice.

With an exquisite sense of purpose he stood the drum on
edge. On that highly polished wood would be painted the scrolls

and mottos and the battle honours. Much good they had done this drummer boy.

He aimed the drum with precision. He moved back a trifle.

He crouched down. By his left side, that nearest the way he had come, lay the body of a seaman. He had been a bosun and his pipe still hung about his neck. Fox cut the cord with a slow noiseless sawing. The whistle was heavy. He waited, peering ahead, straining both ears, both eyes, his nose and every pore of his body, desperate to pick up some warning, some signal – something to tell him when the Indian was on him.

The man on the torture triangle bubbled a sudden shriek and then moaned. The word rustled across the compound.

'Water – *Water*!'

'You'll have to wait, cocky,' said Fox to himself.

He judged that he, for his part, dare not wait any longer.

If the savage was on him when he moved, it would be too late. He could never hope to overpower the primordial muscle-power of the redskin once they got to grips.

Yes. It would have to be – *now*.

He clattered the bosun's pipe across the dirt, let out a muffled exclamation and then thrust hard at the drum. The drum rolled forward paralleling the harsh dividing line between silver moonlight and black shadow.

Back and down, crouching low, his knife in his hand, Fox saw silhouetted against the moonlight the fierce and agile form of the Indian fling itself forward. A single glitter as the tomahawk rose and fell and the drum splintered into matchwood and shredded skin – and then Fox dived, flat, and at full arm's length and thrust his knife into the side of the Indian's belly. He dragged it out, stabbed it in again, struggling to thrust it in and up, again and again. After the first three strokes the redskin was dead.

But Fox struck him a score of times before he paused.

Although it seemed highly unlikely that any more savages lurked within the captured fort, Fox waited before stepping out into the moonlight.

When, at last, he walked out and approached the wooden triangle the man hanging upside down there had his eyes wide open. When he saw Fox he uttered a choked exclamation. Fox cut him free and then collapsed as the man's weight came on him. He dragged himself free, with a curse, and jumped up.

He bent over the two Indians he had struck with his slingshot. The one hit on the temple was dead. The other breathed in a rough and stertorous way, and him Fox mercifully allowed escape to the Happy Hunting Grounds by using his knife.

The white man sat up. He could scarcely speak, and his mouth was a mass of blood.

'Let's get to hell outta here,' said Fox, matter-of-factly. He found a red coat and a pair of breeches he thought might fit and the man dragged them on, with Fox's help, as thought drugged. 'Don't try to talk,' said Fox. 'Those red devils have friends.'

The man, now partially clad, poked around for a pair of shoes. His head was close cropped. He pulled on a pair of stockings, put on the shoes. Fox stripped a piece of white shirt from a corpse and went looking for water. When he came back with a bucket the man simply dunked his head in it. He drew out, shining moonlit drops flying, and looked at Fox.

'Thank you, younker –'

'Don't talk. Them redskins can hear for miles. Come on.'

An expression Fox could not read crossed the man's face, and then he smiled. He looked as though he liked to smile. He was about thirty or so, Fox estimated, with a face at once hard and powerful and yet illuminated by a humanity strange to Fox. His lips had been so maltreated that they had puffed and split and bloodied everywhere; but when Fox gently patted them clean with the wet rag, the man just let him get on with it – his smile had been in the eyes as much as the lips.

He did say: 'I am Ca –'

'No time,' interrupted Fox. Civilians were all the same. They just didn't understand army or navy ways. This man, now, a a sumpter, probably, would go babbling on when all the Indians in America were thirsting for his scalp!

'Cuthbert –' the man said and this time Fox was blunt.

'I'm Fox. We can't stand here all day argifying. I know I'm a boy; but you've got to trust me. Anyway, as a civilian you come under my orders in wartime.'

That sounded good, even if it wasn't strictly true. Fox picked up the tomahawks from the dead Indians, and their knives – two were shoddy trade goods but one looked as though it had a bit of quality about it – and started off for the main gate. 'Come on, Cuthbert.'

Cuthbert's feet were in good condition and they could walk smartly enough out of the fort and down the slope where Fox and his comrades had so laboriously dragged their twelve pounders. The two padded on through the night and presently, as though nature insisted on indicating that she had no part of man's idiocy, the sun started to rise. The false dawn and then true dawn found Fox and Cuthbert well on their way to the next fort in the chain, Fort Shannon.

'If'n Shannon's done fer, Cuthbert, we are in real trouble.'

Cuthbert managed some sort of reply through his mangled lips; but he had taken to not talking, and Fox welcomed that.

A change of outlook had overtaken Fox. It wasn't that he had just killed three men. That they were redskins had nothing to do with it, for they were three brave warriors and they had lost out. But something had stiffened within him during this incident, some fibre had locked into position. He felt very differently from the way he had felt in the aftermath of those two fools in the marsh, Simon and Bruce, and after the inquiry on Mr Doherty. The change he felt and acknowledged. He had taken this tortured man under his orders, acting as though he had every right to order him about. He had forgotten he was just a ship's boy. Something had risen and burst within him and given him a sense of achievement, of purpose, and of an obsessional drive. Just what this new sense was he did not yet know. That it had nothing to do with the glory that was so cheaply touted about he knew with an unshakable conviction.

A low and incoherent cry brought him about. Cuthbert had struck his foot against a branch and fallen. Now he stared up and his eyes were filled with pain, desperate in the early sunlight.

'Easy, comrade, easy,' said Fox.

He had not been stupid enough to overlook an essential item, and he had found it where he expected to find it, in the pocket of the dead bosun. Now he uncorked the rum bottle and tilted it against Cuthbert's lips.

'This is bosun's rum, Cuthbert,' he said. 'That means it ain't watered down with gunk to make grog.' He wanted this civilian to understand that. It was a fact of paramount importance in a sailor's life.

After a short space they started off again. Fox had prodded Cuthbert into resuming the journey with that relentless streak in him that he was aware of only as common sense. It was clear that Cuthbert was in increasing pain. Now they both put their heads down and slogged on. When Fort Shannon hove into sight Fox saw the Union Flag and the scarlet coats of the sentries; but he caught at Cuthbert who was about to rush forward as best he could.

'Wait a minute, Cuthbert. That's what happened at Tarkas.'

How Cuthbert waited Fox didn't know and, with the problem on his mind of worrying about his messmates back in captivity and those bloodthirsty redskins seething to get at them, he didn't much care. After a time and a careful scrutiny, he said: 'Right, Cuthbert. We can heave up the hook and tack in.'

They crossed the cleared space before the Fort and approached the gateway; but long before they reached it a file of scarlet-coated men doubled out, their equipment bright and spotless, to surround them and escort them in.

With a last flourish of the puny authority he had been exercising, Fox said to the corporal in charge of the detail: 'You'd better carry Cuthbert in. He's fair tuckered out.'

The corporal took hold of Fox's ear and shook him.

'An' if you don't keep a civil tongue in yore head, you imp of Satan, I'll pulverise your bottom with my ramrod! Yo hear!'

Fox grimaced. He was back in the organisation of the army – and soon the navy. When he told his news a relief party was immediately organised. Cuthbert had been whipped off to the sick bay. Fox, as was normal, would go back with the redcoats to the relief of Fort Tarkas. His fling of freedom was over.

Chapter Eleven

Conflicting accounts had been received that the great French fleet destined to destroy the Royal Navy in American waters had been observed off the coast of Virginia about to enter the Chesapeake, had actually entered the Delaware, or was to draw all the Yankee privateers into one enormous armada. Eventually, with the arrival on 11th July of *Zebra*, Commander Henry Collins, firm news was received. The Comte d'Estaing with twelve of the line was steering for New York. That afternoon he was observed to come to anchor off Shrewsbury Inlet, four miles from Sandy Hook.

The French were in the war with a vengeance.

The position of the British under Lord Howe was perilous in the extreme. Their small fleet consisted of a few old ships, mostly of light weight and seriously undermanned. Against them the French brought a force now known to be thirteen fine ships, all large for their ratings, and in superb condition. Fox and his messmates discussed the situation from the vantage of their limited horizons, and all agreed that fighting the damn Yankees was one thing; but giving Monsieur Crapaud a licking was another and altogether more enjoyable kettle of fish, entirely.

For one thing, the rebels operated small fast privateers which usually surrendered as soon as stopped and without a fight. Not all did, certainly; but most did. The Yankees had no navy worth speaking of. But the French had, and those fine new ships contained prize money the horny-handed Jack Tars itched to lay alongside.

As it was, the British so heavily outnumbered and out-gunned must set up some kind of defensive front, with the ships anchored with springs on their cables on a line extending from the Hook towards the south western point of the spit. Bomb vessels were placed astern. The incredibly ancient old seventy gun ship *Leviathan* used as a store-ship was given teeth from the artillery park and manned with volunteers.

In these desperate times even Fox found little surprise that the crews of the merchant ships and transports should volunteer. Soldiers clamoured to serve afloat as marines. Lots had to be cast to choose men from the light and grenadier companies to serve, so hot was the desire to go. The shipping agents experienced difficulty in keeping back sufficient seamen to man the merchant ships. The only fly in the ointment as far as Fox could see was the very likely possibility that the Navy would be more than reluctant to see the backs of these fine seamen when the emergency was over and the French thrashed.

No doubt the same thoughts occurred to those higher in the chain of command. Despite his own small-boy cynicism Fox was mad keen to go aboard a ship and get into a good scrap. But the decision was handed down that the *Henrietta*'s men were to be kept together as a crew. Their ship would soon be ready for sea, and then they must be also ready to take her out to lie in the line.

So they manned a shore battery of eighteen pounders and waited for the attack in company with regiments of the army. During this time Fox was delighted to make the acquaintance of an Indian scout, a redskin of a fierce and reckless pride that touched a chord in the scruffy ship's boy. This Indian, who was generally called Red Hawk, Fox met when talking with young Ezra Henry, a Loyal American, serving with the infantry. Red Hawk was an Iroquois, of the tribe of Mohawks, and under the influence of the mighty chief Thayendanegea – 'He placed together two bets' – had joined the Mohawks in their fight against the American revolutionists. Thayendanegea's English name was Joseph Brant, he was educated and held a colonel's commission. So that Fox was mightily impressed by Red Hawk's tales. He did not mention in return his own slaying of three Oneidas in fair fight, thinking with some inwardly-amused shrewdness that Red Hawk would not believe him, would think he merely boasted.

From these days on the heights around the guns waiting for the French to cross the bar and attack, Fox learned much, not least being the tricks and knacks of handling knife and tomahawk. Red Hawk showed him how to throw a knife with such precision that he could cut a human hair at twenty paces.

And – Red Hawk made George Abercrombie learn the knack of throwing with his left hand. As he said: 'You might have your right hand severed by a tomahawk. But that would be no reason to stop fighting, would it?'

Ezra Henry laughed at that, and then swallowed down hard.

But Fox looked at the liquid black eyes of the Mohawk, at the hard planes and ridges of his reddish brown skin, seeing all the strength and tenacity of willpower. 'No,' said Fox. 'No, Red Hawk. That would be no reason to stop fighting.'

The Mohawk tried to give Fox some idea of why pain was of no importance to a warrior. Fox tried to understand. He was oblivious to any reason why the Indian should take an interest in a ship's boy. He had looked with a sharp and intolerant scrutiny at the knife Fox was using. His own knife, the one his father had given him, he kept in his sheath, using the best of the three knives he had taken from the Oneidas. Maybe Red Hawk recognised the knife, understood what might have happened. All Fox knew was that for the first time since leaving the marshes he was not miserable almost all the time.

He was not being unfair to Swede, who remained loyal to shipboard customs. There were other customs abroad in the world. Sometimes sailormen forgot that.

Fox knew how much he owed Swede and was grateful for that. But Swede – no one – could protect him from midshipmen. Rather, those who could would not do so.

When the French fleet finished taking on supplies and water they weighed. Everyone held their breath. This was the moment, this was the time when the British must face destiny, or so they thought, for they were surrounded by enemies. But Comte d'Estaing simply sailed about aimlessly, made no attempt to cross the bar, which would have been best accomplished at nine o'clock, hauled off, hung about until afternoon – and then sailed away south.

It was an anticlimax.

And yet – the Comte d'Estaing and his chief were still on the coast of America and they meant mischief. Fox thirsted to get into another fight. At this time he was all small-boy, and even he could see that the ill-treatment and injustice of his life prodded him remorsely into wanting to take it out on someone – and the only someone hereabouts he would have the chance of giving a bloody nose was the Comte d'Estaing and his fleet.

That the French fleet was greatly superior in size and strength to the English at this time and on this coast meant nothing. If the opportunity of a battle could be contrived then Lord Howe would sail in with all guns blazing, and damn the odds. Already the army were grumbling that the navy was letting them down.

Reinforcements did come in – *Raisonnable*, sixty-four, Captain Thomas Fitzherbert; *Renown*, fifty, acting-captain George Dawson; *Venom*, fifty, Captain Nehemiah Carruthers. Also some of the old hands exclaimed a little wryly when *Centurion*, fifty, Captain Richard Braithwaite, came in. Everyone knew *Centurion*'s story.

Vice-Admiral Byron who was supposed to bring a fleet to the assistance of the hard-pressed navy had still not put in an appearance, his ships scattered by gales. The Comte d'Estaing clearly intended an enterprise against the British in support of the rebels, and this concentration of the Royal Navy was of great assistance to the American privateers. How Fox longed to transfer to a swift sloop or schooner and go chasing rebs!

As it was, *Henrietta* was once more expelled from dockyard hands and set afloat on the ocean. All that meant to her crew was the enormous labour of provisioning and preparing a liner for sea duty.

Previously *Henrietta* would have taken a great deal of time over the process of preparing for sea. Now the *Henrietta*'s tore into the task, unwilling to be left out of the general action everyone foretold. Her bottom was payed over with a poisonous substance of sulphur with a sprinkling of pulverised glass, and then sheathed again – with a soft-wood planking – and payed once more. The theory behind this was that the teredines – the infernal teredo, ship-worm – would eat up the sheathing; but would incontinently be taken with the poisonous cramps and die if they attempted to eat their way through to the English oak beneath.

Captain Shotter, a vitriolic and not soft-voiced man, complained loudly that his ship had not received the system which demanded a layer of pitch covered with brown paper, then another layer of pitch with a massive coating of hair stuck to it, and then having the wooden sheathing affixed with a myriad of broad-headed iron nails. This filling was reckoned to give the teredines a headache when they attempted to eat through the iron nails.

His first lieutenant, greatly daring, said soothingly: 'All those nails give the ship a deuced rough bottom, sir. We'll slip through the water cleaner this way.'

'And the damned Froggies will all be coppered! Damn and blast the scurvy Board of Admiralty!'

Detailed to slave at bringing in supplies, Fox with his mess-mates was hard at work hauling bales and rolling casks and using their muscles until the sweat started from every pore and the average rate of hernia was on the increase. Fox, it is true, was mainly occupied on lighter tasks; but when he saw Swede's massive muscles bulging, and saw Sniffy Billy wipe the back of his hand across his ripe nose and lay on to a rope, and all the time the petty-officers' starters hovering over rounded rumps in taut trousers, he could not hold back from heaving also.

The break for rum when it came was welcome and Swede and Sniffy Billy and the others of Fox's mess threw themselves down, panting, grateful for this short respite. Lofty Green, their mess cook, had trotted off for the rations which would be eaten cold away from the ship, and for the all-important rum issue. Marines prowled everywhere, alert and on the lookout. If a sailor could run from here he would be an extraordinarily clever and persistent man. Nonetheless, some did manage to run.

'Here comes Lofty,' said Sniffy Billy, wiping his nose.

'Ja! Good!' said Swede, and the faces of his messmates showed keen anticipation. Lofty was coming along over the dusty ground bearing the rations – and carrying the rum – and that was what the men's eyes fastened upon.

An abrupt clattering and a yelling and the whickering neigh of startled horses burst into the midday quiet. Fox looked back. A carriage was haring along towards them. Carriages were rare enough in north-eastern America. This one had two terrified horses harnessed to it, a midshipman standing up on the box and lashing the horses on, a bosun sitting at his side and clutching everything in a paroxysm of fear. In the carriage a naval captain and a lady sat, laughing and waving their arms, engrossed in each other and enjoying this madcap ride.

Fox yelled. But Swede's enormous bellow lifted.

'Lofty! Look out!'

The horses roared. The middy laid on his whip. The captain jolted forward on the seat, and looked over the side, his face black with sudden anger.

Lofty tottered. The rations spilled every which way.

Above him he saw the fierce opened jaws of horses, their teeth immense, like animated tombstones. He saw the fire in their eyes. He saw their wicked hooves lashing the air before his face. He yelled. He staggered, not caring about the rations,

And the rum . . .

'The rum!' screamed George Abercrombie.

The rum went up in the air, turned over, came down, and flowed in a seeping untidy puddle into the dust.

The carriage bounded past Lofty, catching him a thwack and sending him spinning. The captain shook his fist. In language that the woman with him would not understand he gave vent to his outraged feelings, threatening all manner of vile and unpleasant things to the blagskites of pimp-faced gutter-louts, call yourself seamen, who had so jolted him and his bride to be.

'The rum!' roared Swede. Sniffy Billy was already down on his face in the dust, his tongue licking at crevices of rum, dust-filled. The others flopped down, their tongues going like flycatchers'; but precious little of the vital fluid remained to be sucked from the dry and greedy dust.

Fox's tongue was barely moistened.

The men sat up.

'The lousy, gold-laced, ponce-faced, creeping bastard!'

'That's Captain Carruthers, orf of *Venom*,' said one of the marines. He looked down at the row of upended seamen's bottoms, as the men lapped desperately at the turpid rum-mud. 'He's getting married termorrer.' The marine saw humour, in the situation. He chuckled deep in his throat, behind his leather stock. 'Hurr! Yore rum's sure rum-dust-pudden, shore is!'

'You red-faced lobster!' Young Billy Mullins started; but Swede grabbed him and hauled him away. Then the bosun arrived with his rattan – a handy cane with protuberant ridges some two inches apart, that dug into a man with painful regularity – and started laying about him.

Smarting, physically and morally, the men went back to

their heaving and hauling.

The incident was no more than that, an incident that merely reinforced Fox's dislike of gold-laced bastards who called themselves officers and gentlemen. That he planned to become one himself, one day, when he was older, had nothing to do with it. That was a matter of necessity and survival. He did not think he could support this hangdog life for very much longer.

The next day Fox went with a gang, escorted by marines, to bring in the last of the supplies. After this only the water remained, always the last to be swung aboard, and then *Henrietta* would weigh and sail.

The sailors trooped along, with Swede and Billy Mullins arguing. The matter was a technical one and Fox listened with both ears wide open. They passed a tavern, and everyone fell silent as a mark of respect to the temple of their faith, and broke into the argument again as they passed a real church set atop a little slope. From the tavern the sounds of hearty laughter came bellowing, and much horseplay. The marines kept their muskets slanted conveniently. Jimmy Ducks said: 'Someone's happy, God rot 'em.'

Outside the church stood a carriage.

The carriage.

Fox said to Jimmy Ducks, who was carrying three chickens and prodding a cow with his stick: 'Jimmy! Let your confounded chickens go a minuit!'

'Eh?' said Jimmy Ducks, his broad bovine face puzzled.

There were no horses harnessed to the carriage and the traces had been removed.

'Drop your bloody chickens, Jimmy!'

'Why, Foxey?'

They were up to the church now, and could hear singing. The tune, as far as Fox could make out, bore some resemblance to a triumphal march suited to the finale of a wedding. He knew little of such matters; but the doors were being opened by a man in a black suit.

In place of the traces of the carriage two pipe-clayed ropes had been hooked on, and both ropes were neatly coiled down, one to starboard, the other to larboard.

Fox gave Jimmy Ducks a push, grabbed a chicken and hurled it at the carriage. The bird managed to become aerodynamic for a few seconds and amid a tumult of russet feathers landed on the box. It started to complain in a loud crow. Jimmy Ducks let the other two go in his startlement and they immediately ran off, squawking.

'Grab them, you bloody idjit!' roared the bosun.

The marines started to laugh. The cow hared off, at an ungainly waddle. The men, taking their cue for a bit of sky larking at the bosun's expense, joined in, and a cheese rolled between the legs of the marines.

'If anyone runs, shoot him!' bawled the bosun, beside himself with rage.

The uproar mounted satisfactorily. Fox had been carrying a broad shallow wicker basket of salad greens, for all these supplies were for the captain's larder and his steward was now running and gesticulating and despairing over this wanton handling of his master's property. The cow nudged into the carriage and the vehicle rocked. Fox put his wicker basket on the ground and sprinted for the cow, jumping between his comrades who were roaring and yelling, dodging colliding bodies. He reached the carriage and then slid down.

He caught a distorted glimpse of the tavern down the slope the way they had come. The carriage pointed that way. The first drag rope unhooked easily. The second resisted him and he yanked harder. It clicked free and he laid the end under the carriage tidily. Then he saw the tavern doors open and a crowd of seamen troop out. They were happy; but they were not drunk. The bosun and bosun's mates with them would see to that. Later, they might drink the health of their captain and his bride. Each man wore a smart red and white striped pair of trousers, and a white shirt. They had straw hats, sennet work, and their neckerchiefs were all blue. They looked smart and fine and dandy, they had cost money to rig out.

They advanced up the hill, shouting jeeringly to the Henriettas who were clearing up the mess. The cow was captured by Fox and brought back to Jimmy Ducks, who grabbed the rope from Fox and planted a wet kiss on the cow's nose, cooing over her like a long lost baby. The cheese was recovered. A marine brought in one chicken. But the other two had vanished and Fox experienced a pious little hope that someone more deserving than Captain Shotter had discovered them.

The sailors from *Venom* were now arranging themselves in

96

two lines at the dragropes they uncoiled. Fox waited, feeling the thick excitement in him like a malignant tumour. If one of them jerked the end too soon . . .

The Henriettas halted at the foot of the slope by an ornamental pool which floated white water-lilies on its green surface whilst the bosun sorted them out. He was enraged. He said to Jimmy Ducks: 'You'll get it, my lad. Oho, yes – Them chickens was paid for!'

Jimmy Ducks said: 'But they flew orf, sir – t'warn't my fault.'

'Don't answer back, goddam you!'

The rattan cut stingingly.

Now Fox felt a twinge. Poor simple Jimmy Ducks. But he doubted that he would be flogged; and, anyway, his mess had two chickens they might donate to Jimmy Ducks to prevent just that. Somehow, Fox knew that the glorious revenge of the Henriettas over the Venoms would not be spoiled by a flogging.

Now Captain Nehemiah Carruthers walked from the church with his bride on his arm. His face was extraordinarily red and Fox surmised he had been getting up Dutch courage for the wedding ordeal. His uniform blazed in the sunshine. The bride looked dumpy in her white bridal dress, with a grotesque erection of flowers and lace adorning her head. Fox recognised her from the incident when they had run over Lofty and spilled his rum.

The first lieutenant of *Venom* saluted his captain smartly.

Fox heard it all.

'All ready to move off, sir.'

'Thank you, Mr Hedges. Very commendable.' Carruthers seated himself in the carriage at his bride's side and waved a negligent hand. The sailors at the drag ropes stiffened. The midshipman on the box released the brake, the bosun at his side blew a resounding trill on his pipe.

The Venoms started off at a smart trot. They must have found hauling very easy. In two disciplined lines they trotted along hauling two empty drag ropes.

Fox put a hand to his mouth.

The Henriettas were looking up the hill at the back of the carriage. They could see the ends of the dragropes trailing over the ground. Someone laughed. Then someone else raised a cheer.

For – for the carriage was moving. But it was not moving

at the pull of two pipeclayed dragropes. It was running backwards down hill. It gained momentum. It ran faster and faster. The two rear wheels, now being in the front, held it straight and the two swivelling wheels at the front, now being at the rear, castored to follow suit.

Down the little slope backwards ran the carriage.

Fox was jumping up and down, now.

The middy on the box was standing up and waving his arms.

The bride was shrieking.

Captain Carruthers was disgracefully roaring mouthfuls of obscene decisions as to the destinies of his first lieutenant, his bosun, the middy, and all his hands.

Down the hill backwards ran the carriage, its wheels all ashimmer in the sunshine.

The carriage hit the rim of the ornamental pool. It tilted and swerved. It toppled over. Captain Carruthers, his bride, the bosun and the midshipman went all headfirst into the water.

Fox had to hold his guts.

Captain Carruthers rose from the pond with a water-lily in place of his cocked hat. His bride, her fine fancy trimmings waterlogged and dripping around her face, her surreptitious make-up dribbling down her cheeks, clung to him, shrieking.

The bosun and the midshipman made great shakes to get the two out.

'My, oh my!' said Swede, on a long breath. 'The Good Lord himself has spoken!'

Henrietta's bosun roared and swung his rattan. He knew when the presence of a great gang of unwashed and chortling seamen was not needed. The Henriettas picked up their gear and departed. They walked with a swing.

Everyone knew.

No one spilled rum and got away with it, not even a gold-laced captain.

Not in George Abercrombie Fox's book, anyway.

Within twenty four hours they had upped the hook and crossed the bar and were on their way to find and fight the whole damned French fleet.

Chapter Twelve

George Abercrombie Fox cursed as an extra wild heave of *Henrietta* threw him against the swinging mess-table.

At one time he would have been tumbling all over the place in the frenzied movements of the ship in the gale; but he had considered he had his sea legs now and could never be upset. And here he was staggering about like a drunk turfed out of a tavern!

The gale must be a sizeable one, then.

Henrietta laboured. Her repairs had not been of the all-embracing kind her age and condition warranted, and already she was working and sea water was flooding the bilges, so that the hands were continuously employed on the pumps. She lay over on her beam ends, corkscrewed, tried to stand on her trucks, ducked her bowsprit green and washed a foaming mass of water down over her forecastle and spuming into the waist. Her storm canvas stood like boards. Men hung on grimly on the exposed decks, and below they hung on just as tightly. Johnny Gumbo's injuries had mended; but no one would forget what the sea had done to him. His once friendly black face was now permanently clouded and vacant from the brain damage he had received.

In the blow *Apollo* lost her main and fore topmasts and her mainmast was badly sprung. Lord Howe had previously shifted his flag from *Eagle* to *Apollo* so as to direct the coming battle with greater flexibility. For two days previously the French and English fleets had sailed within sight of each other without coming to grips. Now this gale had blown the French fleet to the four corners of the ocean, and as far as the *Henrietta* was concerned had similarly disposed of the English, for the next morning nothing was in sight across the tempestuous sea.

A new Master-at-Arms had been appointed, appointed by

warrant of the Admiralty, and he had not chosen to continue Fox in his occupation as servant. So Fox had reverted. He was employed in carrying messages, an extraordinarily hazardous business on the deck that moved violently and treacherously, and on one occasion he overheard Captain Shotter saying with that vicious rasp in his voice to his first lieutenant that the gale had spoiled their chances of prize money.

'We shall have to put back to Sandy Hook, there's nothing else for it.'

'Aye aye, sir. We'll like as not drop our bottom out in this sea. The caulkers can't – '

Then the first lieutenant became aware of Fox, and roared at him, whereat Fox chirruped out his message and departed.

Later on the carpenter went himself to report, moodily, that there was five foot of water in the well and the pumps were barely holding. The rumour went around the lower deck that the ship would have to be lightened, and they all knew that everything of value to the hands would go overboard first, the guns last.

As though by Divine intercession in response to the prayers so blasphemously uttered from the Lower Deck, the gale abated on the following day and *Henrietta* could bear up for Sandy Hook. This kind of termination to an enterprise upon the sea was no novelty; men might build ships and plan what to do and how to do it; but the winds of heaven disposed of all that lived upon the sea. Where the wind blew so would sail the ship, unless she was extraordinarily weatherly and not burdened by a ricketty hull and suspect spars.

Despite his intense hatred of Captain Shotter and the officers, Fox had not failed to note their seamanship and to be impressed by it. *Henrietta* should have foundered; but she had been brought through safely, if badly battered.

Fox possessed a powerful and retentive memory. He had often in the past felt irritation with his family and friends – with Mary, for instance, out on the marshes, or with Harry or Johnny or any member of that old gang in their eternal brushes with the Hogans – that they couldn't seem to remember trivial things or important things. To Fox the custom had by now become habit of assessing experience and of filing it away in a empirical order of importance. He did this sub-consciously now. So it was that in all to do with seamanship and the ways of ships on the seas he watched and studied and learned, and was able instantly to recall exactly the correct piece of information he required.

Fox also had the power of mimicry. He had often made Mary laugh imitating her friends and the people they met.

So now down in the gloomy spaces between the old oaken timbers he imitated Captain Shotter and the first lieutenant and made his messmates chuckle and chortle.

'Avast there, you heathen swabs! Clasp that bowline, curse you for a dung-baby's bottle-snatcher! Shiver my timbers, Swede, you rapscallion of a good-for-nothing lubber! I'll keel haul you and put you in irons, dang you for a scuttle-butt swab!'

Swede, particularly, delighted in these japes of Fox's.

Once, as Fox had been giving a particularly spirited rendition of the bosun in full cry, rousing out the hands to their duty, the next mess along, concealed by canvas hangings, roused out and fled on deck. They believed the bosun had actually come down and rousted them out. Fox didn't believe this at first. But when Sniffy Billy, wiping the back of his hand across his nose, which streamed in sympathy with the tears from his eyes, confirmed the men's sheepish arrival on deck and the tongue and rattan-lashing they then experienced, Fox was forced to believe. And, believing, marvelled.

Already, at twelve years old, almost thirteen, he could perfectly imitate the officers on the quarterdeck. At this time he regarded this as a mere opportunity for a jest. It was all a part of the horseplay and ragging that went on in times of little stress. Now, with the storm dying away in sullen, long-rolling swells, the old ship was slowly coming back to her old routine.

Practising knife-throwing aboard a sixty-four was an occupation fraught with difficulties, and Fox, with considerable regret, was not able to practise as much as he would have wished. He would never forget Red Hawk. He knew that all the Iroquois, except the Oneidas and a few Tuscaroras, had remained loyal to the British. He wondered how they were getting on. He knew enough to know that he could not attempt to evaluate the position. His information was scanty in the extreme. This, too, he admitted was a prodding source of discontent, even at his age, and a fruitful cause of his strengthening resolve to quit the lower deck.

There was no doubt whatsoever in his mind that he would leave the Lower Deck and the Forecastle, and claw his way aft through the hawsehole and stride the Quarterdeck with a telescope under his arm and a gold-laced hat on his head, a sword at his side. This was a mere matter of growing up. There would be things it would be needful to know. So he took the most ferocious pains at learning everything he could. He now knew every part of *Henrietta*, and could find his way about her blindfold.

As part of his plans, which although in the final outcome were a hardly-formed as granite were, in the immediate details, vague in the extreme, he made sure he got on to good terms with the Gunner.

Guns and gunnery fascinated George Abercrombie.

He was as agile as the monkey for whom he and his boy comrades were named as he practised the duties that would fall on him in action. In addition, he studied all he could of the handling of the great guns. He asked questions. He studied. He was never satisfied until he had the point at issue absolutely clear in his mind.

Captain Shotter, although a hot-tempered man with a vicious tongue, was wise enough in sea lore to make sure his men knew how to handle guns. Gunnery evolutions were carried out with the same intolerant attention to perfection as were sail evolutions. A ship might carry the smartest topmen in the navy, and shake out her sails and sheet them home in the quickest imaginable time; but if she could not manipulate her batteries with a corresponding skill, then all the rest was a waste of time.

On the following day wind and sea had so far moderated as to make life once more reasonable. Sea routine once more claimed everyone aboard *Henrietta*. She might be only a tiny sixty-four, old-fashioned and under-manned; but for all that everything that had to be done according to naval regulations must be done, and done in double-quick time and to perfection. Fox learned quickly that only perfection would be tolerated.

'Sail ho!'

At the lookout's call everyone came to a fresh expectancy. It was probably only another British ship like themselves driven off station by the wind and now bearing up for Sandy Hook. It might be an American privateer. In that case the sail would have no interest at all for *Henrietta* for despite her newly-payed bottom she could not catch a fleet privateer. The schooner or whatever she was would simply range up and have a look and then, as though lifting her skirts at them, hoist canvas and veer away with the wind, laughing at them. The third possibility was the one that fascinated.

When the white triangle, tiny and shining, lifted above the sea rim, all those who could do so crowded to the rail to watch and to offer sage comments on the identity of the stranger. *Henrietta* had already altered course. The white scrap over the horizon grew in size, and changed in shape, and shone in the sun, and approached and came nearer and presently Swede thumped his fist down and said: 'A Froggy! I'd bet a week's rum on it, ja, I would! A verdammt Frenchman!'

In immediate confirmation of Swede's words the marine's drums roared through the ship and the boatswain's pipes twittered. Fox felt the thump of blood through his heart.

'Beat to Quarters! Clear for Action!'

Every soul aboard had a job to do and the members of the chain of command, from the captain down to the lowest ordinary seaman, would see that the jobs were done. Right at the bottom of that ladder stood the ship's boys. There was no one they could tell what to do. Not even the women, for many of them had had long sea experience.

The wind swept smoothly across the decks. The sun shone. The sea stretched broad and glittering, heaving gently. And *Henrietta* moved sedately across that wide shining expanse, her reason for existence now suddenly thrown glaringly before every one of her company.

Fox knew his tasks and as the drums roared and the pipes shrilled and men hurried to their action stations, he went methodicaly about sloshing water and sand on to the decks. When the decks were fully wet and sanded, so that men would not slip, he went about filling the buckets with water. Sea water in which the rammer would thrust the sponge to make sure no dangerous sparks were left within the gun barrels, and fresh water – or what passed for fresh water aboard ship – for the men to slake the raging thirst that possesses a man in action amid the smoke and fury.

'Step lively there, lad!' roared a bosun's mate and – *thwack!* went his colt against Fox's straining rump. Fox concentrated on what he was doing and didn't even swear.

He had his guns and his section of the deck serviced.

He saw Joey likewise occupied, and others of the ship's boys. They were a bare-footed, raggle-tailed bunch; but they ran with a snap and an alacrity that scarcely needed the extra incentive of a mate's starter.

All this was mere preparation, of course, on a par with the men's occupations in readying their guns, and fitting chain slings to the yards and preventer stays, and rigging nets, all the minutiae necessary for a ship going into action.

The thought that perhaps the Frenchman might be a frigate and simply sail away and there would not be a fight filled Fox with so profound a choking sensation that he refused even to contemplate it. There was going to be a battle! There had to be!

Swede was tying a red kerchief around that yellow mop of hair, curling up the small pigtail. Sniffy Billy was doing the same. Both were stripped to the waist.

'Remember, Swede, like always,' said Sniffy Billy. 'We takes each other's dunnage, if one o' us gits plugged.'

'If a round shot takes orf yore head, Billy, it'll be a certain cure.'

Fox was interested to see that although all the men were serious in their demeanour and a few of the more religious persuasion were repeating prayers, there was a general feeling of levity, of the approaching apocalypse, when all normal restraint upon their conduct would be removed. The men's faces were grave, and they prepared for battle; but beneath it all the wild lilt of blood surged them on, willy-nilly.

They all knew they would win in this action. Any other thoughts did not occur to them.

The temporary partitions had been struck down from aft and carried below and now the gun decks lay open, from bow to stern, with all obstructing impedimenta cleared away. The surgeon and his loblolly boys and the purser were below, preparing canvas in which to carry the wounded, and spreading blankets to receive the living who might soon be dead, and buckets in which to carry away portions of anatomies that might be cut off.

Big Ben – the Liverpudlian with the enormous hernia – was trying to buy a gill of rum, and was offering fantastic prices. Fox heard him go up to a guinea, and then left to go about his work. Had he a gill of rum he would have sold it and struck a bargain on the spot – or would he? Maybe a belly warmed with a shot of rum might not be a bad thing at this moment. But, George Abercrombie was kept far too busy to think about the reality of the situation.

He saw Mr Midshipman Lafferty abusing Timothy, the boy who had once been servant to Mr Doherty. Lafferty was not content merely to strike Timothy, who cowered away; the midshipman actually kicked the lad, foully, and Timothy had to accept this abuse, as Fox had accepted it many times, without a single remonstrance. A murmur, an objection, any sign of rebelliousness were the very reactions sought by Lafferty. Then he would pounce. The offending man would be triced up at the gangway, seized by his wrists and his knees, to receive a red-checked shirt. In the case of Timothy, a boy, he would be thrown bare-bottomed to receive a caning over the breach of a gun.

Those great guns themselves were now cast off, the tompions removed, and carefully loaded.

'Triple-shot the brutes!' roared the first lieutenant, and the men seized the round shot from the garlands. Fox had brought up his first wood and leather bucket of cartridge to his gun. He repeated the exercise for the opposite gun where Sniffy Billy as the second gun captain would take over if required. The order to run out the guns was not given.

Slushy, who had been Swede's second gun captain, had got into a fist fight with Hairy Joe when they'd been ashore in New York, and had decided to leave the mess, as was his right. He was a good man and had been rated as first gun captain on Number Eight gun, and Sniffy Billy had taken his place.

Now Hairy Joe looked back at the quarterdeck, frowning.

'Why'n't they run the guns out?' he said to Thomas Smith the Fourth. There were six Thomas Smiths mustered.

'Go an' arsk the capt'n, Joe.'

'Haw!'

Alfie Trotter, who serviced Sniffy's guns, bumped into Fox as they passed on the deck.

'Watch it, Foxey!'

'If'n you gits in my way agin, Young Alfie, you'll git knocked flying.'

But there was no great animosity in the exchange. Like them all in the ship, the boys were keyed to a tight expectancy of what was to come which left little room for purely personal bickering.

The glaring exception to that, as always, was Mr Midshipman Lafferty.

True to a tradition that could only mean anything in circumstances like those in which the men now found themselves, Lofty Green, he who had been so disastrously knocked over by Captain Carruthers' carriage and lost the mess's rum, shook hands with Jock Macintosh. The two men had been enemies sworn, getting on each other's nerves as is sometimes the case between men for no apparent reason. Now Lofty and Jock shook hands on the eve of action.

'If'n you's kilt, Jock, I hope you go to Heaven and not the place I always swore you'd a go to.'

'Aye, mon. An' if you're tumbled o'er, I hope it's aisy for ye.'

Fox knew what that meant, what Jock had previously wished, and he approved; but also and with the natural cynicism of a denizen of the lower deck he guessed the two men would be at each other's throats after the action – if they both lived.

Fox had been so busy as the ship came to preparedness that there had been no time to rationalise out the cause of all this hustle and bustle. *Henrietta* moved sedately through the water under topsails and topgallants. The courses were clewed up. Chains festooned the yards, all in carefully planned arrangements to catch a shattered spar and to prevent too much debris from falling on to the spread nets and the deck beneath.

All the ports of the lower gun deck shielding the batteries of twenty-fours and those of the main deck shielding the twelves remained closed. Noise reverberated and echoed like manic churchbells within the long open spaces of the lower gun-deck; but Fox was accustomed to his place within the ship and the noise, although magnified, was nothing to worry him.

His guns, being on the main deck and in the waist, presented the advantage that he would from time to time be in the open air and could see what was going on and also the disadvantage that the enemy tended to concentrate their fire on the waist. As he scampered up and down the ladders, he was so engrossed with what he had to do that this latter consideration weighed little with him.

The Gunner and his assistants in the magazines and powder rooms were the ones for whom the battle would be merely a succession of shocks and sounds. This, Fox considered, weighed very heavily against any desire on his part to become a Gunner. At least, as he intended to be an officer, he would be spared that. As it was he snatched his charges from the handlers crouched over the screens with alacrity and scampered off. He wanted to get back to the maindeck and see what was toward.

The gloom of the lower gundeck gave way to Atlantic sunshine and he blinked a couple of times before he saw, looking aft, the form of Captain Shotter standing by the quarterdeck rail.

Captain Shotter was doing his duty by tradition and giving the hands a short and rousing call to action and duty. He made it brief. Vicious though his tongue was, intolerant though he might be of slackness and indiscipline and all the other evils emanating from the lower deck and befouling the high ideals of the quarterdeck, he could yet animate the hands. Many of them swore by him. A taut captain, they told Fox, is the right sort. You know where you are with him. 'At the gangway, getting the cat!'

Now Captain Shotter bombasted about the French, and about the English always winning.

'And if any man jack of you doesn't do his duty I'll have him triced at the gangway and I'll take the skin off his back! You'll all stick to your posts! The marines know what to do if any of you blagskites tries to skulk off! And keep those guns firing! God Save the King!'

The men broke into a cheer.

To his intense surprise and chagrin, Fox found himself joining in.

Everything to be done had been done. Now absolute silence was ordered. Silently save for the eternal noises of a ship at sea *Henrietta* glided on. The wind blew cheerfully and the sun shone benignly. The blocks clattered and the timbers of the old ship groaned at each surge, the thrum of the rigging was muted and the canvas whispered in the breeze.

Now Fox could look overside.

He saw the approaching Frenchman.

His first impression was of size.

'My God!' he said to himself. 'She's a big 'un!'

George Abercrombie Fox was only a ship's boy at this time, although the word only is a poor descriptive. He knew little of the greater world. But he did recognise this ship sailing so arrogantly towards them under topsails and top gallants as a large liner. He stared, drinking in the details of her appearance.

Swede whispered from the side of his mouth: 'She's a bigger yin than a seventy four. Ja! She's an eighty!'

Captain Shotter had *Henrietta* running middling free with her yards practically at right angles to the line of the deck. Had he wished to run away he would have had to wear ship and bring *Henrietta* around on to the larboard tack and sail as close-hauled as the old ship could manage, the yards braced hard over. The Frenchman was closing them off their starboard bow, beating close-hauled on the larboard tack. A feather of white lifted and broke from her bows as she plunged through the seas. If the weather worsened and even a tiny outrider of the past gale blew back the Frenchman would have to let her head pay off a trifle, and then, again, perhaps Captain Shotter could wear *Henrietta* and escape.

The wind did not shift and the seas remained calm and no thoughts of running away entered Captain Shotter's head or the skulls of anyone aboard *Henrietta* – at least, so Fox thought, keyed up to the coming fight.

Now Fox found he was doing a simple calculation in his head. He could estimate the rate of *Henrietta*'s passage through the water with exactitude – she was doing about seven knots, although Fox did not calculate from that base but rather from time and distance to be covered – and from the same estimation of the Frenchman's speed and course he could map out in a two-dimensional plan the exact point at which the two courses would intersect if no helm orders were given, and the times at which both ships would reach that vital spot.

He saw, quite clearly and with no possibility for error, that the Frenchman would cross *Henrietta*'s bows at killing range. The Frog would rake them before they could fire a shot in return!

If Captain Shotter decided to put his helm down and bear around in order to bring his larboard batteries into action that would mean only that *Henrietta* would have to face the full shattering broadside of the eighty. And if the English captain put his helm up, wearing away, in the attempt to cross the Frenchman's bows, the answer to that manoeuvre would be a reciprocal movement from the Frenchman letting his head pay off, so that his larboard still bore.

George Abercrombie Fox, at the same time as he gained an inkling of what being an officer might entail and the life and death decisions it would bring, also felt the terrible fascination of these calculations. They appeared to him, a mere ship's boy, like a drug of the most satisfying kind. Just to stand up there aft on the quarterdeck and have all this great floating fabric of wood and canvas and iron guns, and the minds and bodies of these flesh and blood men, under his command and subject to his will! To calculate. To make decisions. To take the risk that was based on knowledge and skill! Not to gamble, but to know what to do and how to do it, and work out the odds, to add up the pros and cons, to decide through a maze of complicated calculations what best to do to save oneself and destroy the enemy!

No other form of gambling, no other form of mathematics, no other form of desire, appeared in those closing moments as of any worth to Fox. He knew, now, that this was what he wanted. This was his life. This cool calm appraisal of a highly technical situation, pitting his wits and skill against the brains of another professional – yes, this was what he wanted!

Captain Shotter had a foul and vicious tongue. But he was a seaman. He was a professional fighting sailorman. He had an old and small sixty-four to pit against a new and large eighty. The odds were immense. Fox stole a glance aft.

Shotter stood calmly, his hands tucked into the small of his back, gazing across the closing gap at the Frenchman.

And Fox knew.

He knew what he would do.

And he guessed Captain Shotter would do exactly that same thing, too.

When the captain opened his mouth and bellowed his orders, adding a fine string of obscene verbiage to accompany them, Fox felt the pure glow of absolute passion for an abstract and erudite art flood him.

Right or wrong, he and Captain Shotter had made the same decision.

Henrietta's sail trimmers roared into action. The ship moved with the action of wind and water, surging and rolling, with a great slatting of canvas and a squealing of blocks, the smack of bare feet on the white holystoned decks loud.

And George Abercrombie Fox was carried forward willy-nilly, a ship's boy, into the smoke and flame of action, one of a crew of Davids contesting with a crew of Goliaths.

Now there was no drawing back – and George Abercrombie Fox knew that he would not wish to be anywhere else in all the world.

Chapter Thirteen

Henrietta's head paid off, she surged directly before the wind. Fox knew that if neither ship made further alterations to their respective courses, *Henrietta* would just scrape past the Frenchman's bows. The French captain could not allow that. He could not come up further into the wind, for then he would be in irons, and helpless, so he would have to let his head pay off, swing with the wind, give up his chance of raking the British ship from bow to stern, and engage his larboard broadside with *Henrietta*'s starboard.

Fox watched the Frenchman's canvas.

He saw the yards swing and he yelled, all alone, a boy's voice shrilling in the disciplined silence: 'Helm alee!'

'Silence, you scum! Bos'n! Take that man's name!'

But Fox was already gone, disappearing below the hatchway where only those entitled to pass were allowed through by the marine sentries. After a moment, he bobbed back. In all truth, in this moment, no one was going to pay any more attention to a ship's boy than to see he did his duty and ran with his powder and refilled the water butts and did not skulk in a corner.

They were rushing down upon the Frenchman.

Just as Fox had calculated, just as he had so impetuously shouted out – as though he, a ship's boy, was the captain! – *Henrietta*'s helm had been put down and she had rounded like a hunting dog square on to the starboard tack. The Frenchman had swung away to save himself from being raked, just as Fox had guessed he would, and *Henrietta* was swinging back and hurtling down on him. It didn't matter now which way the Frenchman turned. Larboard or starboard, his tall ornate stern, with its encrusted galleries and wide windows glittering in the sunshine, all lay open to the ferocity of *Henrietta*'s larboard broadside.

The French eighty towered above them.

Her sails shone in the light.

She bulked immense, seeming to rush towards them in the impetuosity of their own progress. Fox found his hands were gripped into two knobbly fists, and he forced himself to slacken the constricting grip of his muscles. He watched, absorbed, fascinated, completely caught in the rapture of this scheming and calculating.

Now the glassed stern of the eighty bulked over them and they were swinging again under the nudge of their rudder, the sails left now to take care of themselves in this climactic moment.

'As you bear, Mr Fairweather!' roared Captain Shotter.

'Aye aye, sir!' roared back Mr Fairweather, the third lieutenant, in command of the maindeck guns.

Now *Henrietta*'s bowsprit inched past the stern of the eighty. She was reaching on her, sliding past, the wind cutting across her decks and across the scrap of water and against the Frenchman's stern. She was attempting to swing, now; but that manoeuvre was far too late.

Mr Fairweather at the foremost larboard twelve-pounder gave the necessary order and: Crash! The first gun fired. Brownish smoke jetted. The second gun fired. The rippling concussion smashed its way down the deck. The lower gundeck twenty-fours joined in with their deeper note.

The noise of the trucks on the wooden decks added their rumbling to the din.

Looking out, in the instant that he thrust the powder charge into the hands of the waiting gun crew, Fox saw the ornate stern of the French eighty. He saw the name splashed all across that stern, emblazoned in gilt. But, he could not read. The name meant nothing to him.

By the time he had completed his next mad dash down the hatchway and along the deck to the wooden screen over the magazine and received the cartridge thrust through the hole by a muscular arm and then hared all the way back *Henrietta* had passed the Frenchman.

Most of the powder monkeys concentrated on running with their cartridges, thrusting them at their gun crews and then of hurtling across the deck and down the hatchways to the powder room for more. Fox did all this. But, in addition, he took note of what was going on.

Henrietta, having passed the Frenchman, now had her full on the lee beam and could put her helm up and so curl neatly into position on the Frenchman's starboard quarter. Fox chalked one up for Captain Shotter.

Someone was yelling in the din. Smoke blew streaming away from the English ship, partially obscuring the French eighty, so the decks remained clear. The marines were firing at the high transom, and Fox saw heads up there, and the spurt of smoke, and knew the French soldiers were shooting back.

He heard the name of the Frenchman, now, for the first time. *Saint Lunaire*.

Saint Lunaire, an eighty, was a hundred and eighty feet on the gundeck, thirty feet longer than *Henrietta*, longer than many a British three-decker. Her beam was fifty feet, six feet more than *Henrietta*'s. She towered above her smaller antagonist, her lower deck gunports riding high above the water whereas the sixty-four would have difficulty in operating her lower tier of guns in anything of a seaway.

On *Saint Lunaire*'s lower gundeck she carried thirty forty-two pounders, and on her main deck thirty eighteen pounders. Her forecastle and quarterdeck mounted twelve-pounders. That weight of shot could blow *Henrietta* out of the water.

On any scale of calculation *Saint Lunaire* possessed more than twice the fighting weight of *Henrietta*. She would also inevitably have more men aboard, for the English ship was as usual undermanned, having no more than four hundred and fifty men and boys – plus the women. The Frenchman would probably have eight hundred or so men and soldiers aboard. The contest was going to be severe.

At the moment, *Henrietta* was having it all her own way.

Those first raking broadsides must have smashed their way through *Saint Lunaire*'s stern, gone rampaging forward dismounting guns, destroying men, blowing everything away before the triple-shotted discharges.

And now a fact on which Captain Shotter had gambled and which, until it was explained to him, Fox could have had no knowledge, came into play to the advantage of the English. It was the custom of the French Navy at this time when going in to action to clear away only the broadside which would be engaged. The captain of *Saint Lunaire* had clearly anticipated taking his larboard broadside into action. Thus all the lumber and gear which on British ships was stowed away below or flung overboard had on the French eighty been stacked up between the guns on the side they had expected not to be engaged.

Now *Henrietta* glided down the Frenchman's starboard side and poured in a massive series of blows to which she received only a last faint and feeble reply.

The last two forty-two pounders fired.

What they did shocked Fox into a realisation that he was in a fight very different from anything in the shape of fisticuffs.

The mizzenmast of *Henrietta* came tumbling down.

A wild confusion of canvas and sheets, blocks and tackle, rained down. The chain preventers would have held the yards; but the mizzen was ripped through below the top and everything above swayed and toppled and tore down through the nets. Captain Shotter, wiping blood away from his forehead, roared obscenely and kicked men into hacking away the wreckage.

Fox, on his wild chase down to the magazines and the reckless dash up the ladders to the guns, cast a glance aft and saw the shambles there. *Henrietta* was wearing to come around; but the loss of her mizzen hampered her and she would not answer the helm.

In desperation, Shotter let her fall back and as once again the iron mouths of the guns hammered out their broadsides the old sixty four leaned in towards the spanking new eighty. Now gun muzzles roared and flamed across the gap.

Everyone gave an answering cheer to the French, who had set up a shrill caterwauling when the English mizzen fell, as the Frenchman's maintop tottered, swayed, and then fell.

Now the marines were peppering away. Fox saw one of them fall backwards, off the gangway, and sprawl in the way of the gun carriage as Swede applied his linstock.

The twelve-pounder belched flame and smoke and smashed back. Her tackles were hardly necessary. The scarlet-coated body of the marine, already dead, provided a shock-absorber.

'Get the poor bloody lobster out of it!'

Men seized him and hoisted him and over the side he went, his black hat rolling stupidly on the blood-splashed deck. Fox took a single look and was hurdling down the ladders again for fresh powder. He just had not taken the incident in.

On his way back he saw a twenty-four pounder abruptly rear

up, daylight breaking in through the bizarrely enlarged port. The gun flattened its crew and slewed across the deck. Then Fox was up the ladder and on to the deck and into the outer uproar. Now brown smoke wafted everywhere, chokingly. He saw a seaman staggering towards the hatchway, his face hanging down, an eye dangling, his mouth a half-moon of blood. The marine sentry let him pass.

Joey was running past Fox when he stopped, looked stupidly at Fox, dropped his powder, said: 'Oh, Foxey!' coughed a great gout of blood and dropped, dead. Only when his comrade sprawled face down on the deck could Fox see the ghastly hole punched in the lad's back.

'Powder, you black bastard! Powder!'

Fox ran.

Swede ducked his face into the bucket of water that was swimming with coils of greasy blood. Water was water.

Suppose, thought Fox, suppose Swede has his blond hair all smeared with blood, his head knocked off, his guts torn out?

No. That couldn't happen.

A tearing noise like a manic scythe sweeping across the deck made Fox jump. A round shot had passed above, high enough not to damage. A line parted and dangled. Smoke wafted.

The British guns fired very rapidly. Very rapidly indeed. Everyone knew that was their only chance, the only way they could outfight these damned French. The big forty-two pounders were clumsy pieces, slow in action; the British put in two broadsides to the French one. Just how long they could keep it up would depend on many factors. As Fox jumped over a sprawling seaman who shrieked with what was left of his face and skidded on blood and raced down the ladders, he found himself, with no trace of any feelings of macabre ghoulishness, working out rates of men dead, and of energy expended, and of triedness, and of the probable effect on the French gunners in *Saint Lunaire*.

He felt a sense of being cheated every time he had to run below deck for powder. He wanted to be up on deck, in the open air, choked as it was with gunsmoke, working out chances. There, he felt sure, lay his destiny.

Back on deck he saw Swede roaring his gun crew on. Sniffy Billy lifted his hand in the old familiar gesture to wipe his nose and Fox saw that hand miraculously disappear and Sniffy Billy wipe a stump across his face that smeared greasy blood brightly over nose and lips and cheek.

'My Gawd!' said Sniffy Billy. His wrist pumped blood.

The third lieutenant whipped out a handkerchief – it was white and freshly laundered – and bound up that wrist and as he did so he was yelling with a near incoherent shriek: 'Fight your guns, you bastards! Fight! Fight!'

The deck at Fox's feet abruptly splintered and split and he was tossed over, his powder in its case flinging around and crashing into his side. With stubborn persistence he gripped hold of the strap and did not let go.

Lofty Green, in the act of hauling the gun in, staggered back and looked down and saw his intestines pouring out. He gripped them in both hands. He looked puzzled. He died before they could get him below.

Over on the hatchway Johnny Gumbo was sitting with that idiotic grin on his face. The marine sentry yelled at him, then prodded him with his fixed bayonet. Johnny Gumbo sat on. The marine pushed him.

'Hey! Johnny! Look alive!'

Johnny Gumbo, with that fixed lunatic look on his face slowly keeled over and fell.

He was dead. Very thoroughly dead. A passing roundshot although not touching him had done his business for him, had finished what the gale had begun.

Fox was up and down the ladders and up again, staggering as the ship bucked under the combined thrust of her own guns and the awful punishment she was taking from the great guns of *Saint Lunaire*. The insane bedlam racketted on in smoke and flame.

Now that Joey was gone and Alfie Trotter, too, cut into two pieces, Fox had to service three guns. The cartridge case gave protection against sparks, and to carry bare powder was asking for trouble; so Fox seized Alfie Trotter's case and swung nimbly bare-footed up the ladders carrying both. He was taking a chance; but there was a battle raging above and he must bear his part.

The next time he came on deck a party of men were hurrying aft. They carried boarding pikes and tomahawks and cutlasses. From aft there came through the din, faintly, the shriek of dying men and the spluttering of small-arms fire as the muskets cracked before the bayonets came into play. Fox could see little there through the smoke; but the French were trying to board!

His duty was to bring powder. He did so. But he wanted to snatch up a boarding pike and hurl himself at the throats of the French.

The insane activity boiled up to a crescendo. Belting along from the wooden screen swinging his two cartridge cases, Fox stumbled across Bully Travis. The boy had avoided Fox since he had been put in his place. Now he half sat, half sprawled across the cables. His cartridge case lay at his side. He was sobbing. Fox halted.

'Hey, Bully! Step lively!'

Travis looked up, his big face gaunt, his eyes swollen, the tears thick on his cheeks. He was trembling wildly.

'I can't! I can't go up there agin!'

'Course you can, Bully! It's better up there, ain't it, than dahn 'ere! Wot's got inter you? It's — '

'I ain't agoin' up there! They can flog me all they like!'

Young Billy Mullins ran past.

Fox stopped him.

'You take Bully's powder up, Billy.' Billy Mullins did not argue. If any lads argued too much with Fox these days he would deal with them. Fox slapped a hand hard on Bully Travis's shoulder.

'You service Billy's guns, Bully. Twenty-four pounders, mind. So remember at the screen. Now, jump to it!'

Fox hefted the bigger lad up, pushed him towards the magazines, and kicked him up the rear to assist him the better.

'We've got the Froggies to beat, Bully! You mind that, too!'

On deck again into the inferno he got a lungful of smoke and coughed. The deck of *Henrietta* was in a dreadful state. Dead men lay sprawled in their own blood, the living too busy to hurl them overboard. He could catch a glimpse of the masts of *Saint Lunaire* and could count two – bad cess to 'em! He ran to his gun and saw that Hairy Joe was still working the gun although an ominous stain of blood spread all across his left shoulder and his arm hung helpless.

Swede was still yelling encouragement and working like a demon. He was still safe, then!

'Where you bin at, Foxey?'

'Here Y'are, Swede – gotta git to Ted Armitage's gun.'

'Ted's dead. A splinter big as yore arm degutted 'im.'

Swede swung back into action again. The noise made hearing difficult; but Fox was picking up the knack of it. His head might ring; but he was learning to sort out words from the maddening thunder of the guns.

At Ted Armitage's gun the three men left were working the piece as fast as they could. Fox passed his powder over and ran off and slipped on a patch of blood. His foot skidded through the greasy sand and he tumbled over. His head hit the deck an almighty wallop and for a moment he lay there, seeing stars shooting through his head in time to the bellowing of the guns. From here he could look up and see the havoc in *Henrietta's* rigging. Every sail was a sieve. Yards had been ripped away, lines hung entangled, and he judged that at any second the main-topmast would go. He lay there a moment, feeling the pains clawing his skull.

As he sat up he saw Mr Midshipman Lafferty, his face as white and green as mouldy cheese, stride towards him. Lafferty's fists were clenched and they trembled against his sides. He was quite out of control.

He kicked Fox.

'Get up you cowardly scum! Little toad! I'll have you punished for this!'

Fox scrambled up.

The midshipman was gibbering at him, spittle drooling from the corners of his mouth. His eyes were blank and glazed.

He kicked Fox again. His hard polished shoe hurt.

'I'll have you beaten over a gun, you toad, you whoreson! I'll see you get it – '

Mr Midshipman Lafferty stopped speaking.

He fell down.

He had no legs.

Blood pumped out across the deck and as he lay there his jacket twitched and Fox realised a musket ball had penetrated his belly. The midshipman shrieked. Fox bent down.

'Serve you right, you black bastard! I hope you rot in hell!'

The midshipman's glazed eyes took on a look of one already roasting. He spoke, something about a flogging, a curse, and then he shrieked something quite unintelligible.

Fox glanced up.

As he had suspected, the maintopmast, shot through and its stays and shrouds shot away, toppled and fell. He jumped back, shouting a warning. He looked at the midshipman.

Lafferty was gazing at him with a look of utter terror.

Fox laughed.

Then the maintopmast struck the deck and obliterated Mr Midshipman Lafferty. A thin pool of blood oozed from the splintered timbers.

The inferno raged on.

Amid the smoke and the cries and the smashing concussion of the guns time meant nothing. How long had they been fighting? Fox did not know and he did not care. He just wanted to beat the eighty-gun *Saint Lunaire* and then take an enormous drink of rum.

He had slaked his thirst with the blood-fouled water. Now he seized an opportunity to replenish the butts. The fire from *Saint Lunaire* slackened a trifle, he fancied. He could see only one mast left and wondered when the other had gone.

The seas moved the ships, fast locked together. More than once the French attempted to board and were met with musketry, fire from the swivels, and grape, and then in the clash of naked steel were driven back. Marines were taken from their stations at the guns to strengthen the parties repelling boarders, but the fire of the British sixty-four miraculously continued in a drum-roll of fury.

Noise. Noise. Noise.

Smoke and more smoke.

Continual running, up the ladders with the powder, down again to fetch more. On and on. Over and over again. Sliding on the brains of Samuel Rawlinson, one of the white mice who would never snoop and pry again. Slipping on blood. Running up on deck with powder, and running down again – and then running back. On and on and on.

The first lieutenant passed along the deck heading a body of marines and seamen, bristling with weapons. He was shouting, but in the din Fox heard only: 'Stick to your guns, lads! The Frogs can't stick to theirs!'

To his intense surprise, Fox felt this to be true. Such had been the intensity of the fire from the English guns that despite the greater calibre of the French pieces the French gunners had been quite unable to keep pace and were now reluctant to carry on shooting. The noise sensibly decreased. The occasional shattering bang as a forty-two pounder belched sounded strangely loud. The smoke drifted away leeward, a dirty-brown man-made smear over the surface of the sea, extending for miles before it dissipated.

Now Fox could see the deck from the knightheads to the taffrail. He found it difficult to understand. It was as though some giant maniac had stirred everything on the deck with an equally giant spoon. The shambles was shattering in its completeness. Only the stump of the mainmast was left; the rest of it must have fallen after the topmast finally cleansed the world of Lafferty, as Fox phrased it, and spars and canvas and ropes tangled everywhere. The boarding netting had been ripped to shreds. Hatch coamings were riven and splintered. The quarterdeck looked as though it had been rubbed with an enormous holystone, levelling everything, and the conceit of that image gave Fox a sense of fitness.

Captain Shotter, his head bandaged, the blood staining the cloth, was raging and yelling back there, and here came the first lieutenant and his men. There were fewer now, and some were wounded; but now Fox could see the cause of Captain Shotter's choleric concern.

Up there the quarterdeck of *Saint Lunaire* loomed hugely. The scend of the sea had swung the ships so that now their quarters touched. No ship could lay exactly alongside another for the shape of their waists and the tumble-home; but the quarterdecks were almost touching now and the French were massing in a final effort to make use of their vast superiority in numbers. They would board and carry the fight on to the blood-splashed decks of the English sixty-four. They would compel her to strike, for, Mon Dieu, there would be no English left to resist.

Mrs Thomson appeared at the hatchway carrying powder.

She had been servicing the guns for a long time now. Once, going past below, Fox had seen her calmly binding up a man's thigh. Where his lower leg and foot were God knew.

'I'll keep Swede busy, and the others, Abe. Do you cut along aft. Take a boarding pike.'

Fox, for the first time for a long period, felt dubious.

'My job's here, Mrs Thomson.'

'The Frogs will be aboard if'n you don't help! D'you think I want to be raped by a crew of an eighty! A damned fifty would be bad enough! Be off with you!'

Still carrying his powder Fox ran aft. He had some wild and crazy notion in his head already.

The English twenty-four pounders continued to beat out with deadly precision and at these close quarters their punishment was like that of a prize-fighter who slugs away at his opponent's midriff. They were tearing the guts out of *Saint Lunaire*. Indeed, most of the French forty-two pounders had fallen silent. Their maindeck twenty-four pounders still fired but erratically. Smoke wafted uneasily over the decks. The blood patches on the scrubbed and sandied planking caught vagrant gleams of sunlight and bronzed to a slick shine.

Fox reached the quarterdeck. A seaman lay on his face with no legs and only one arm. Fox picked up the boarding pike near his, holding it in his right hand. He had climbed up on to the quarterdeck by using hand holds and footholds in the splintered wood, for all the ladders were smashed. Had he picked up a weapon earlier he would not have been able to climb.

Captain Shotter was shrieking above the din.

'Shoot the rascally Frenchmen down!' A string of sea oaths. 'I'll not have a damned Frog on my quarter deck!'

Up on the low poop the fife rails were completely missing and the upper edge of the taffrail looked as though it had been nibbled away. The first lieutenant and his party were awaiting the onslaught of the French, who were massed above them and ready to jump.

The marines stood back and picked off their men, biting their cartridges and loading and ramming with a phlegm that Fox, even in that mad moment, had time to admire.

This was the supreme test. If the French gained a lodgement there were enough of them to push the Henriettas into the sea.

The choking, constricting and suffocating sensations of the past hours – for hours they had been fighting – lifted for Fox. Now he could, as it were, take a grip on the whole situation. He was nearly thirteen, short still, as he would always be, but broad and deep through the chest, and he possessed muscles that could drive a boarding pike through a man's guts. He would play his part in repelling boarders.

In those few moments as he reached the shattered quarter-deck the peculiar overview he had of the action resolved itself into an understanding that the initial punishment *Henrietta* had handed out with those first raking blows and the subsequent hammering of the Frenchman's side, cluttered with lumber between the guns, had given the little sixty four just a chance, a slender chance, true; but a genuine one. All below decks had been swept and scoured by the huge roundshot of the forty-twos. The main deck had been brushed by a broom of fire. But the Frenchman had lost enormous numbers of men, and far from obtaining a quick victory over her smaller antagonist, had caught a wildcat by the tail. If this last boarding attempt could be beaten back the moral victory would be with the English, and then they might battle through to the real victory itself, however crazy that might have seemed.

And now George Abercrombie felt with a driven shock the memory of old Chalky's wild tales of how *Monmouth* had taken *Foudroyant*. Those lurid yarns had been one cause of his joining the navy. Well, his dreams had not turned out as he had expected; but he could have no complaints over this yarn. None at all!

Twice the enemy set foot on the deck and twice they were repulsed in the sleet of grape and canister, of fire from the swivels and the slashing musketry of the marines – and in the rush and thrust and stab of the hands with their cutlasses and boarding pikes and tomahawks.

And, now, for the first time events lost their precision for Fox so that the world turned into a chiaroscuro of twisting bodies and the flash of fire, the screams of men and the scraping clash of steel, the anger and the violence and the sheer persistence that would not own defeat.

He found himself clawing up the ornate side of *Saint Lunaire*, following the first lieutenant whose white breeches and stockings were befouled with blood. They were on the Frenchman's quarterdeck. A few soldiers ran before them. Smoke obscured all the forward part of the eighty; but it was drifting and dissipating, lifting and shredding. Fox looked forward.

Through the thinning veils of smoke he saw three masts and trim sails, all standing, rigging in perfect condition, the masts broadening and he did not, for a moment, comprehend. Then he realised this was another ship.

Another ship!

There had only been two ships in all the world. There could only be two ships – *Henrietta* and *Saint Lunaire* – there could not possibly be another ship! It was unthinkable.

Then the smoke puffed and the newcomer, a frigate, poured in a broadside that raked through *Saint Lunaire*, bow to stern, a broadside that signalled the end.

After that it was a matter of the fleur-de-lys coming down and of the Union Flag being hoisted, of the French captain handing his sword to Captain Shotter, of a quietness that hurt the ears. It was perfectly natural that the tars who had won the victory should stand quietly to witness these final moments. The captain of the frigate came aboard and expressed astonishment at the shambles and the destruction, and he caught Shotter warmly by the hand. 'Magnificent, my dear William, positively magnificent! This is a great day for you and *Henrietta*. I am proud to offer you my most sincere congratulations.'

Fox gaped.

His jaw hung down.

Some of the French wounded had not yet been cleared off *Saint Lunaire*'s quarterdeck and now a movement there caught Fox's eye. As a boy he had been standing a little to one side of the hands, and they all knew that at any moment they would be chivvied back to their own ship and the colossal task of making *Henrietta* seaworthy would begin. After the action came the real hard work. But now Fox turned. A French soldier with half a face and a single eye that blazed with madness was lifting himself on his left arm. In his right he held a pistol. That pistol pointed at the group of English officers, at the back of the frigate captain. Only madness could have made the Frenchman behave like this, the intolerable pain of his wound, the sense of defeat and the fact that he was a soldier and not truly of the sea. The pistol muzzle centred on the frigate captain's back.

Captain Shotter let out a cry. They all turned and froze as the pistol muzzle covered them.

Fox drew the knife his father had given him and as Red Hawk had taught him threw.

The knife buried itself in the French soldier's wreck of a face and completed the work the canister had begun. The pistol exploded and the ball cracked harmlessly aloft.

No one else had moved.

Captain Shotter roared.

'Boy! C'mere!'

Obediently, Fox walked across and as he had been taught knuckled his forehead.

'That was quick thinking, lad. And I saw you in the boarding. A smart younker – what's your name?'

Fox said: 'Begging your pardon, sir, Fox.'

But he was looking at the frigate captain with the gape-jawed look so uncharacteristic of him.

He could not stop himself. He could no more have held back his tongue than he could have lifted *Henrietta* on his back.

'*Cuthbert!*'

'What's that?' Shotter's face turned purple. He braced himself up, opened his mouth – and the frigate captain spoke.

'The devil take me! William – I do believe – bless my soul – this is the young devil I told you of! Fox! Yes, that's right – well, trice me in a hammock with a roundshot! If that ain't the deuce of a strange turn!'

All Fox could understand was that this gallant frigate captain was Cuthbert, the naked, tortured by Indians, civilian sumpter he had taken out of Fort Nahan. Incredible.

This was Captain Cuthbert Rowlands, captain of His Britannic Majesty's thirty-two gun frigate *Nicodemus,* a very well-thought of officer and one destined for high flag rank.

Fox stood there, a miserable raggle-tailed ship's boy, and wondered just how many thrashings the boatswain would hand out for this.

Captain Shotter, indeed, was clearly about to order some unpleasantness for Fox when Captain Rowlands, with a smile that Fox found disturbing and reassuring, all at the same time, intervened. 'From what you tell me, my dear William, he is something of a young fire-eater. I believe I could find him a place in *Nicodemus* – with your permission, of course – more suited to his undoubted talents.' He gestured to the dead French soldier now being carried away by French prisoners. 'I saw his work with a knife on those confounded Indians. It seems that I owe young Fox my life twice over.'

Rowlands took Shotter by the arm, a familiarity showing they were friends in addition to being captains together on the list, and walked him away. As though that were signal enough the activity began of refitting the two ships and of making them capable of undertaking the passage to Sandy Hook. Men were still bringing up the dead from the aft cockpit and hurling them overboard; that would stop now and eventually the slain would be given a decent burial at sea. With the feel of the declining sun on his cheeks and the air now breathing fresh and smoke free, Fox suddenly and with a great and genuine sense of thankfulness realised he was still alive.

The two captains returned and Fox stood before them.

'I cannot do anything for you, Fox,' said Shotter. 'I've enough damned followers as 'tis. So thank your lucky stars Captain Rowlands is taking an interest in you.'

That was the word – Interest.

'I'm taking you in *Nicodemus* now, Fox. But you'll have to stay and help set up *Henrietta*. As soon as that is done, bring your dunnage aboard. I will speak to you then.'

With that, Captain Cuthbert Rowlands turned and went aboard his own ship to order out parties to assist the Henriettas.

Clambering back down the gashed and splintered side of *Saint Lunaire*, walking across *Henrietta*'s quarterdeck, slipping and sliding down to the maindeck, going down the ladders to the lower gundeck, Fox found he could not understand clearly what had just transpired. He did know that his life had changed. He did understand that he had come into possesion of the greatest gift a seaman must have if he is to progress in his career. He had Interest. Without Interest a sailor was nothing, mere thistledown floating on air. He mused with a quite un-Fox-like uncertainty about what the future might hold.

He saw Swede with a great sense of thankfulness that his friend and mentor was still alive. He would say goodbye to Swede now. So many he had said goodbye to, so many messmates and comrades, of the old *Henrietta*.

Yet, he must think ahead. He had come through a profound and illuminating experience, and he would never be the same man again, a dividing line had been set between his boyhood and his manhood. All manner of subtle and treacherous thoughts clawed at his mind. If he could continue on this course, with the Interest of Captain Cuthbert Rowlands, the way lay open to the Quarterdeck. There would be the business of learning to read and write along the way, of course, and mathematics and all the other imponderables that were stuffed into officers' heads.

He had known he would be an officer one day.

The sun was slanting into the western horizon now and the sea stained a brilliant bronze and orange sheened and shot through with viridian streaks and magenta swirls. The sky rioted in umbre and rose and crimson.

Now he could look forward with some confidence to returning home – if his head wasn't taken off by a roundshot – and seeing his family and jingling gold pieces in his pockets. His future seemed to him assured. He renewed that old intolerant vow, that obsession, that no one and nothing would stand in his way.

The future beckoned with gold and glory, opening up with promise, roseate with fame and fortune.

George Abercrombie Fox would never be satisfied; but he could sense the beginnings of achievement. He had a long way to go; but this start he had made was not at all a bad one for a humble Thames marshboy, brought forth into this world by his uncle's hanging, and born in the gutter.

NEL BESTSELLERS

Crime

T013 332	CLOUDS OF WITNESS	*Dorothy L. Sayers* 40p
T016 307	THE UNPLEASANTNESS AT THE BELLONA CLUB	
		Dorothy L. Sayers 40p
W003 011	GAUDY NIGHT	*Dorothy L. Sayers* 40p
T010 457	THE NINE TAILORS	*Dorothy L. Sayers* 35p
T012 484	FIVE RED HERRINGS	*Dorothy L. Sayers* 40p
T015 556	MURDER MUST ADVERTISE	*Dorothy L. Sayers* 40p
T014 398	STRIDING FOLLY	*Dorothy L. Sayers* 30p

Fiction

T013 944	CRUSADER'S TOMB	*A. J. Cronin* 60p
T013 936	THE JUDAS TREE	*A. J. Cronin* 50p
T015 386	THE NORTHERN LIGHT	*A. J. Cronin* 50p
T016 544	THE CITADEL	*A. J. Cronin* 75p
T016 919	THE SPANISH GARDENER	*A. J. Cronin* 40p
T014 088	BISHOP IN CHECK	*Adam Hall* 30p
T015 467	PAWN IN JEOPARDY	*Adam Hall* 30p
T015 130	THE MONEY MAKER	*John J. McNamara Jr.* 50p
T014 932	YOU NICE BASTARD	*G. F. Newman* 50p
T009 769	THE HARRAD EXPERIMENT	*Robert H. Rimmer* 40p
T012 522	THURSDAY MY LOVE	*Robert H. Rimmer* 40p
T013 820	THE DREAM MERCHANTS	*Harold Robbins* 75p
T018 105	THE CARPETBAGGERS	*Harold Robbins* 95p
T016 560	WHERE LOVE HAS GONE	*Harold Robbins* 75p
T013 707	THE ADVENTURERS	*Harold Robbins* 80p
T006 743	THE INHERITORS	*Harold Robbins* 60p
T009 467	STILETTO	*Harold Robbins* 30p
T015 289	NEVER LEAVE ME	*Harold Robbins* 40p
T016 579	NEVER LOVE A STRANGER	*Harold Robbins* 75p
T011 798	A STONE FOR DANNY FISHER	*Harold Robbins* 60p
T015 874	79 PARK AVENUE	*Harold Robbins* 60p
T011 461	THE BETSY	*Harold Robbins* 75p
T010 201	RICH MAN, POOR MAN	*Irwin Shaw* 80p
T018 148	THE PLOT	*Irving Wallace* 90p
T009 718	THE THREE SIRENS	*Irving Wallace* 75p
T013 340	SUMMER OF THE RED WOLF	*Morris West* 50p

Historical

T013 731	KNIGHT WITH ARMOUR	*Alfred Duggan* 40p
T013 758	THE LADY FOR RANSOM	*Alfred Duggan* 40p
T015 297	COUNT BOHEMOND	*Alfred Duggan* 50p
T010 279	MASK OF APOLLO	*Mary Renault* 50p
T015 580	THE CHARIOTEER	*Mary Renault* 50p
T010 988	BRIDE OF LIBERTY	*Frank Yerby* 30p
T014 045	TREASURE OF PLEASANT VALLEY	*Frank Yerby* 35p
T015 602	GILLIAN	*Frank Yerby* 50p

Science Fiction

T014 576	THE INTERPRETER	*Brian Aldiss* 30p
T015 017	EQUATOR	*Brian Aldiss* 30p
T014 347	SPACE RANGER	*Isaac Asimov* 30p
T015 491	PIRATES OF THE ASTEROIDS	*Isaac Asimov* 30p
T016 951	THUVIA MAID OF MARS	*Edgar Rice Burroughs* 30p
T016 331	THE CHESSMEN OF MARS	*Edgar Rice Burroughs* 40p

T011 682	ESCAPE ON VENUS	Edgar Rice Burroughs	40p
T013 537	WIZARD OF VENUS	Edgar Rice Burroughs	30p
T009 696	GLORY ROAD	Robert Heinlein	40p
T010 856	THE DAY AFTER TOMORROW	Robert Heinlein	30p
T016 900	STRANGER IN A STRANGE LAND	Robert Heinlein	75p
T011 844	DUNE	Frank Herbert	75p
T012 298	DUNE MESSIAH	Frank Herbert	40p
T015 211	THE GREEN BRAIN	Frank Herbert	30p

War

T013 367	DEVIL'S GUARD	Robert Elford	50p
T013 324	THE GOOD SHEPHERD	C. S. Forester	35p
T011 755	TRAWLERS GO TO WAR	Lund & Ludlam	40p
T015 505	THE LAST VOYAGE OF GRAF SPEE	Michael Powell	30p
T015 661	JACKALS OF THE REICH	Ronald Seth	30p
T012 263	FLEET WITHOUT A FRIEND	John Vader	30p

Western

T016 994	No. 1 EDGE – THE LONER	George G. Gilman	30p
T016 986	No. 2 EDGE – TEN THOUSAND DOLLARS AMERICAN		
		George G. Gilman	30p
T017 613	No. 3 EDGE – APACHE DEATH	George G. Gilman	30p
T017 001	No. 4 EDGE – KILLER'S BREED	George G. Gilman	30p
T016 536	No. 5 EDGE – BLOOD ON SILVER	George G. Gilman	30p
T017 621	No. 6 EDGE – THE BLUE, THE GREY AND THE RED		
		George G. Gilman	30p
T014 479	No. 7 EDGE – CALIFORNIA KILLING	George G. Gilman	30p
T015 254	No. 8 EDGE – SEVEN OUT OF HELL	George G. Gilman	30p
T015 475	No. 9 EDGE – BLOODY SUMMER	George G. Gilman	30p
T015 769	No. 10 EDGE – VENGEANCE IS BLACK	George G. Gilman	30p

General

T011 763	SEX MANNERS FOR MEN	Robert Chartham	30p
W002 531	SEX MANNERS FOR ADVANCED LOVERS	Robert Chartham	25p
W002 835	SEX AND THE OVER FORTIES	Robert Chartham	30p
T010 732	THE SENSUOUS COUPLE	Dr. 'C'	25p

Mad

S004 708	VIVA MAD!	30p
S004 676	MAD'S DON MARTIN COMES ON STRONG	30p
S004 816	MAD'S DAVE BERG LOOKS AT SICK WORLD	30p
S005 078	MADVERTISING	30p
S004 987	MAD SNAPPY ANSWERS TO STUPID QUESTIONS	30p

NEL P.O. BOX 11, FALMOUTH, TR10 9EN, CORNWALL

Please send cheque or postal order. Allow 10p to cover postage and packing on one book plus 4p for each additional book.

Name ....

Address...

....

Title ....
(SEPTEMBER)